G R E E N

T H U M B

ANNIVERSARY EDITION

GREEN · THUMB

TOM
CARDAMONE

ISBN: 978-1-59021-759-7

This book is a work of fiction. Any references to historical events, real people, or real
locales are used fictitiously. Other names, characters, places, and incidents are products
of the author's imagination, and any resemblance to actual locales, events, or persons
and plants, living or dead or mutated by genius box, is entirely coincidental.

to the

boys

in the

sand

INTRODUCTION
TREBOR HEALEY

Green Thumb, deservedly awarded the Lambda Literary Award in 2013, is a singular gay novel. There's nothing quite like it; this fascinating dystopian adventure stands out for the ease with which it deals with sexuality from the perspective of both the author and the characters we come to know. Praised by critics as "eco-erotic," "lush," "weird," "unsettling," and plain "holy sh*t beautiful," it is all these things and more, busting out of any single genre. Like the novels of William Burroughs, which it has the most in common with, this book is as chimerical as its characters, many of whom a mysterious magical device called a genie box (implicated in whatever disaster brought civilization to an end) created: a hybrid world of pelicans with humans hands, boys who are half-skate or reptilian, along with the book's hero, Leaf, some kind of plant, fed by light, unable to feel pain, and possessing a healing ejaculate to all who partake of his stem during the numerous orgies that place in the course of the story.

Yes, this is a dystopia, and yet Cardamone infuses his wet world with a beauty and possibility that invites the reader to consider different ways to think about progress, hope, time, and evolution, as well as dystopia itself – not to mention sexuality and communion. His descriptions are lush: beautiful passages about the sea, mangroves, and swamps; detailed depictions of architectural innovations among the ruins; down to the food its denizens eat; and an overall pregnant-with-danger yet joyfully Brueghelian medieval ambiance to the little cobbled-together towns featuring with the those most Burroughsian of characters, the tattooed and thieving diveboys, reminiscent of Burroughs eponymous novel, *Wild Boys.*

Because the challenges of life are so elemental in this tale—with its themes of survival and comfort and trusting others—I am reminded of another great dystopian novel set in Florida, *Fiskadoro.* The late Denis Johnson echoed that there will likely always be some consolation, a kind of good riddance, to certain aspects of so-called civilization. Florida certainly speaks for itself in this regard.

Populated by beings who have returned to an earthier culture, close to nature, with no qualms about embracing the sensual, *Green Thumb* offers readers something of a central love story. However, the sexual expression of its characters is never restricted and is essentially polyamorous, an organic outgrowth of joy and community. Whatever variations in gender or orientation come up are all treated as natural and accommodated as such, if noticed at all.

But ultimately, *Green Thumb* is the story of a journey, first with two boys and then four, some being chimeras and one of whom has lost his father, which sets the stage for a quest. As they travel through what is left of the flooded Florida Keys on their way to a ruined Miami, they have to avoid "slavers" and the usual powerbrokers who exploit and separate people for their own gain and control, reminding us that even after the apocalypse some things never change: put your faith in the meek, for Leaf has a destiny unimaginable, profound, poetic, and mind-blowing, suggesting a future that is as inconceivable as it is utterly thought-provoking.

Why am I not surprised? Because I first met Cardamone in the early part of this century at a bar that had emerged from a converted massage parlor on the Lower Eastside called Happy Endings. The irony was not lost on anyone as Cardamone read one of his fascinating stories ("Suitcase Sam," a wildly imaginative deconstruction of gay male sexual excess).

After that fateful meeting, I proceeded to read everything he'd written, delighted to find dozens of fantastical tales in his story collections, *Pumpkin Teeth*, and *Night Sweats: Tales of Homosexual Wonder and Woe*, many like "Blue Seaweed" with very happy endings indeed, and his series of novels— *The Werewolves of Central Park*, *Pacific Rimming* and *The Lurid Sea*— that are to a one all boldly queer and never what you'd expect.

Cardamone is a true original, a writer I'd been looking for without even knowing I was doing so. In Green Thumb, Leaf describes Hardy as a boy who "tasted of tomorrow." I think we can say the same of Tom Cardamone, who has given us a novel—and an oeuvre—that is indeed eco-erotic, lush, weird, unsettling, and plain holy sh*t beautiful. *Green Thumb* provides a superlative introduction to this profoundly original and visionary writer's mind.

TREBOR HEALEY

TABLE OF CONTENTS

PART

ONE

EVERY ANGEL
IS TERRIFYING

RAINER MARIA RILKE

ECSTASY

ONE AFTERNOON I HELD MY green hand up to the sun and watched as the rays pierced my fingers until they were translucent. I spread my fingers wider and started as a shape stepped between me and the sun. This sixth finger remained, and I closed my palm, shielded my eyes, and sat up. A boy, a sunspot of a boy, with black skin and tight curly hair jeweled with sea foam and white bits of sand and shell. Water beaded off his shoulders, and his chest swelled with heavy, patterned breathing. His body was compact and muscled. A filthy white loincloth kept a tentative grip between his legs. His limbs looked like they could shoot from his body like spears. We studied each other. This dark child of the ocean surveyed the island, taking stock of the dilapidated house and the surrounding waters. Satisfied that all was as it appeared to be, benign, no place for pirates or slavers, he spoke first.

"You live here alone."

"Yes."

He came closer and looked me up and down, his face a feral mask.

"Are those your crab traps on the beach?"

"Yes. But you can have them; I don't need them anymore."

"What, you don't gotta eat out here?"

"No."

"So you fish?"

Twin bracelets of fishing line wound around each of his wrists.

"No."

"So, what do you eat?"

"I eat sunshine."

The boy looked across the bare dunes, the wisp of an island, and the lapping ocean.

"Well, out here, that must make you a millionaire."

ISLAND

LEAF LAY BY THE BARREN, cracked swimming pool. As the sun peaked, he reclined on a battered lawn chair, mouth open, arms out, legs wide apart, basking in the light, the calmness, the nourishing peace. A cloud passed. He stirred from his harmony and rolled over to take a sip of captured rainwater. When the sun returned, he was again prone, fingers spread, neck extended.

He flowered.

Light poured into his open mouth, down his throat, illuminating every chamber of his heart, setting bones aglow. The boy's green skin never peeled or flaked from this constant exposure.

The white petals around his neck uncurled like yawning cats. The shimmering hair on his head was uniformly short (he never had to cut it) and slightly darker than his vegetable flesh. It clung to his skull like clover on a blustery cliff. Slight but sharp blades of grass furrowed into matching question marks over his eyes.

These eyes were deep pools of gold. Central dark gems shimmered in their depths. A singular leaf clasped his loins.

Uncounted years ago, when Leaf was an infant (not that he could remember much of his seedling years, his fearful parents, though dimly he understood that thunder bellowed like bombs), his father came to his crib one night. Delighted and desperate, his father hovered over the sleeping baby, a small case in one hand, the nanny nervous at his shoulder. The light from passing police cars and ambulances painted the room hysterical, patriotic hues. He pulled on his beard and righted askew glasses. "Son, I have a gift for you."

Leaf woke. Like any child, he liked gifts and brightened, though he was puzzled, the dross of sleep clinging like a silken cobweb. His father opened the case and removed what at first looked like a clunky, old-fashioned rotary telephone. The thick cream-colored cord spiraled toward what appeared to be a thin microphone, but the shiny head was sealed. His father held the device up for closer inspection: the dial had symbols instead of numbers. The symbols were an evolutionary array, the machine a prototype. The house shuddered. From another room, his mother wailed, and his father fell toward the crib, his fingers caught in the dial of the device. The wand went sailing, and the horrified nanny stumbled to intercept it as it bounced off the baby boy's head. The child quizzically tried to cross his eyes and contemplated whether this strange episode deserved a good cry. On the floor, his nanny gurgled and moaned, caught in the cord of the humming machine and cocooned in the glow emitted by the wand. A leg in loose stockings shook. His mother made the doorway, nightgown disheveled—a bundle of clothes across one arm, an open suitcase dangling from her other hand.

Crying was in order, but before he could wind up his whimper and tears, the cobweb of sleep tightened like a gentle but insistent net; the darkness of the night became a heavy cloak. The nightlight blossomed from the corner of the room like a radiant yet distant succulent. He reached for this marvelous beacon, but his whole being hummed like a tuning fork.

This was the start of the Red War. Chaos engulfed the world.

The boy and his nanny were whisked southward to the safety of the family's vacation home, his parents to join afterward. They never made it. Ever since, though, Leaf has been reaching for that light.

THE POOL WAS FILLED WITH sand. When not beside the pool, Leaf combed the beach. Tall cattails whispered against his bare thighs as he hiked the shifting dunes. The sun massaged his green shoulders.

Whenever the sun hit a part of his body previously unexposed, a nutritious jolt of energy engorged every cell therein. He had long admired, with no small amount of jealousy, the brown, radial heads of the cattails. They seemed liberated, bobbing beacons that absorbed celestial light equally from all sides. Their perfection made his movements of veneration feel awkward and unsatisfactory. He longed to be a blind flower, rooted, unaware that he cast a shadow.

His best friend lived in the ocean. The thousands of pitched reflections of sunlight tickled at a distance and, upon contact, offered inebriation. Leaf couldn't swim. The distillation of sunlight in water acted like a narcotic; if he waded too far out, he was in danger of floating away in a stupor, then eventually dissolve into a wavering mass of seaweed. The ocean offered only drunkenness and a deathlike drift. He often wondered if that was what dreaming was like. At nighttime, he died. And was reborn with every dawn. At night Leaf never dreamed. Dreams were for the day when infused by the sun's rhythm, he closed his eyes and measured the sunspots erupting ninety-three million miles away. A wind of furious luminosity flirted across his cheeks like a typical breeze. A snap and wrinkle in space that could scorch the world registered as a delicious ripple across his closed eyelids.

His friend Skate lived underwater. He flittered along the seabed, his whole body twittering above the shifting sand, the breaking water; he scooted silver minnows into his underlying mouth. Someone in Skate's previous life had also gotten hold of a genie box. The equipment must have aged so much that the symbols were worn off the dial—its gifts were now a lottery. A blessing or a curse, fins or feathers, gelatinous mass or rock of calcium with a lone human eye at the pinnacle that cried diamonds. On Skate, the genie box had bestowed aquatic compression.

He would glide—an undulating leather angel beneath the surf, safe from the lingering effects of Ebola bombs and undetonated hornet missiles. The boy was nearly two-dimensional.

All from the wave of a wand.

Skate possessed beautiful, ever-inquisitive eyes on top of his head, the faint impression of eyebrows pulled back as if even he were surprised by his shape and circumstance (which gave him the air of a good listener). They often talked for hours, Leaf thinking Skate rapt with attention when such stillness encouraged flighty minnows to draw close. When his emerald friend was about to make a point, Skate would triumphantly suck in the nearest little silver fish. Ever since they had met, when a rogue wave momentarily beached a stunned Skate and Leaf eased him back into the water, they had established a unique language of eye and body movement. Leaf mused about the island, how the house was crumbling, and the eternal, soothing sun. Skate rippled his responses and rolled his eyes. His tales were epic tales: how he had fought off agitated octopi, his curiosity toward aloof female rays that idled in the shallows of a certain sandbar. He talked about fish and fishermen and what he could glean about the occupants from the undersides of their boats. Leaf listened, sometimes with a sense of disbelief that there were other people in the world, that they valued things other than sunshine. On such days he reminded himself that he had known and loved one of them countless years ago.

OF THE MYRIAD REMAINING KEYS dangling below Florida, what remained of the island Leaf occupied was far from the thin residual spread of humanity. Rising tides and whistling missiles had depopulated much of the South. Here the remaining "salts," so nicknamed because they made their living from the sea, lived hard. Proud members of the Conch Republic, without any memory of their forefather's secession from the United States of Wreckage, they fished in deep and dangerous waters and clung to whatever land they could claim, from mere specks of sand to the remnants of broken bridges.

Leaf's small island was surrounded by vast shallows. Long sandbars stretched in every direction. The wooden houses that once populated the island had long since been pulled apart by erosion, though skeletal road signs surfaced during low tide to hint at shredded landscapes, an underwater cemetery of forgotten foundations eaten by coral and crusted with clam. The island was ringed by dunes, bolstered by a struggle of dry grass surrounding the lone structure still standing, a storm-battered two-story Victorian house that had grayed and blistered beneath the relentless sun in the decades since the war. A box of shadows forever empty. Tomato plants had filled the windows when the house was a living home. His nanny had napped on the porch.

A few years ago, the porch was dragged out to sea during a particularly fierce nighttime storm. (Years? Leaf did not keep time nor fully understand it as the thought, the theory, the ghost of it reminded him of yet another laundered shadow, a dark shoal where tidal memories gathered and dispersed.) As the sandbars amended themselves, so did the island shift; the house now stood perilously close to the water. When he was much younger, a driveway and a road flowed into the surf. Sand had since covered both. And Nanny was gone.

Nanny had worn a broad-brimmed hat and a frayed powder-blue paisley handkerchief tight across her nose, obscuring her mouth, behind which an unusual jaw worked a lisping kindness and wisdom. Her slow, thick speech hinted that she might have more teeth than necessary. She was old even when he was at his youngest, stooped and fragile yet sharp and active, and she kept that gray house together. Boards and shingles stolen by hurricanes were dutifully replaced with driftwood deposited by the same storm. Rusted tubs expectant with stout watermelons crowded the now-waylaid porch. Potatoes pushed against greasy cylindrical glass jars. Every surface was given over to life-sustaining horticulture. Nanny complained that the watermelons were brackish, nothing like the scarlet sweetness of the fruit from her youth. Leaf wouldn't know. He never took a bite, waving her off and turning his nose up. It would have been an act of cannibalism, she understood. As the boy lay by the pool, she would collect rainwater from an old sail stretched across its concave surface.

He helped her cultivate the fruits and vegetables, rotating them for maximum exposure, delicately measuring their ration of rainwater. She said that she had never seen better tomatoes and, acknowledging the adverse conditions, exclaimed that he must have a green thumb. She laughed at this and never tired of repeating it.

On mornings they walked the shore and enjoyed the breeze while gathering driftwood and marveling at the odd debris.

"Too bad I can't come up with a use for all these singular shoes," she often said.

They found bottles, too, dentures, and even a human skull with a crisp bullet hole in the center of its forehead. Once, as a joke, Leaf planted it in the sand on a makeshift post after they found a beaten tin mailbox. Nanny would pause as they walked past and stare into its empty, barnacled maw, the black hole a well of forgotten grief. One afternoon at high tide, as she slept fitfully on the porch, Leaf pushed it back into the hungry waters.

ON THE HOTTEST DAYS OF summer, when the earth was closest to the sun and Leaf heard his song, he rose and slowly began to spin. Emerald dervish, the ring of white petals at his neck like wings in the air, he spun. The sand and concrete beneath his feet receded. He waited, savoring the moment before he smiled and let the light weave between his teeth and coat his mouth.

Sunlight gripped his dark green tongue like a handshake—two dignitaries from separate worlds meeting for the first time, establishing trust and trade. His gums fumed with delight. Nanny had told him that his high noon antics made him look like a lion silently roaring at the universe. But Leaf instinctively knew that he was more the dandelion, about to shake apart in ecstasy—white petal mane sifted by solar wind, its happy echo of nothingness resonated.

Nanny told her green ward about the world and how it was.

And as he grew (yes, yes, yes, like a weed), Nanny weakened. She tried to teach him to read and write by scratching symbols in the sand with a stick. No matter the lesson, he would smooth the sand with his hands, draw the sun, and smile when it was his turn. Conceding that his language was more extensive than hers, she told him of the night and about the moon. He could only see the moon those afternoons it made itself available, low on the horizon, a prehistoric clamshell eroded by sky. To her, the darkness was something personal. Leaf found it foreign, another country. He had seen the border at dusk and had no chance or desire to cross over. But she spoke of the night with an obvious longing; a silent sigh would lift her mask slightly. She would pull at a strand of her hair absently when she talked of the night and the world and how it was.

As Nanny's hair grayed, a single, sturdy leaf grew to grip Leaf's crotch, guarding his newly lengthened stamen. Nanny walked more and more slowly, hunched. Sometimes they walked the receding perimeter of their island just once before she needed to rest when previously they had circled it several times. Leaf knew what the moon represented to her: it was the city, all of the cities, a vast metropolis of promising towers, white marble, unbroken windows, clean statues, and vast bridges that arched toward heavenly dreams, everything good before the war that was now forever out of reach.

Nanny grew more forgetful, and Leaf tended her vegetables and pulled in the crab traps. Occasional storms left the house battered, and he did not know how to make the necessary repairs. She said that this was okay, that she never went upstairs anymore. The porch sagged, and the shadows deepened.

ONE MORNING ON THEIR WALK, they rounded a bend in the beach and discovered a mammoth sea turtle dead. The wind blew its stench out to sea so they could get close. Neck extended, a heavy, notched cranium sunk into the sand. Seagulls had pecked out the eyes. A swollen tongue forced open its mouth; sea lice swarmed the dry crevice. Leaf had never seen a turtle before and marveled at its size and shape. The dull spokes of barnacles studded its shell in dry streams of indecipherable acrostics, marking eons of drifting wisdom. One flipper was missing—gristle poured out of the socket. The boy turned to Nanny, about to speculate shark attack, but she had sunk to her knees and clutched the moist sand, crying. She looked at the eyeless wonder and wept. Placing a trembling withered hand on the creature's shell, she moaned and searched the vacant sky.

Leaf was confused and scared and hated the majestic corpse for bringing Nanny to such a state.

He led her back to the porch when he felt she could stand. He brought her a steeping cup of his special homemade tea (the kitchen possessed a wood-burning stove, and though he always stumbled with the matches, the lighting of the kindling, those dry and vegetable bones, never struck him as ghoulish).

She smiled weakly at him and asked for a blanket, even though it was already late morning and quite warm. After she had some soothing tea and had fallen asleep, he grabbed a paddle that had washed ashore long ago and marched down to the surf, determined to push the dead thing back into the water, but the rising tide had already done its duty. Nothing remained.

A smear of seaweed, a black scurry of sea lice, and a random wisp of flies, an indentation in the sand soon smoothed over by the unremitting waves.

NANNY GREW WEAKER AND WEAKER. She stopped going for walks and stayed on the porch. Leaf struggled to prepare her meals.

Crushing a crab from one of the traps seemed vulgar, and he was guiltily grateful when she spurned his half-hearted attempts to prepare meals. Her speech became more labored. She napped most of the day. During their last trip to the shore, a defiant leathery fin broke through her blouse between pinched and rounded shoulder blades.

Leaf grew lethargic within the shade of the porch. As his eyes closed, she would hum nonsense, or songs from her youth would make her cackle, which would make her cough.

One morning he woke with dawn's light, and she was dead. The next day seagulls found her and picked at her but eventually left unsatisfied. The morning sun that bathed the porch hardened her skin. The tomatoes withered and died, though the aloe spread wild, and its limp obstacle course filled the kitchen. Her clothes rotted. The handkerchief blew away, revealing three rows of massive interlocking shark teeth, a permanent smile of sharp bone. He thought of putting her out to sea like the turtle but felt the porch was her home. Leaf pulled the largest tooth from her brittle jaw and fashioned a necklace with a bit of twine. She remained on the porch until, years later, a midnight storm swept the island and pulled the porch, and her with it, out to sea, leafleting gray shingles from the roof up and down the beach.

As dusk crept across the horizon, Leaf settled into his rickety lawn chair by the empty pool and smiled while thinking of Nanny. Fingering the tooth, he found its serrated curvature soothing. It was the arc of a comet, wind-whipped palm frond, the knife no one sees coming.

WHEN SHE DIED, LEAF STOPPED growing. For years he walked the shore every day in her memory, circling the island. That was where he eventually met Skate. Skate was his best and only friend until Scallop strode ashore.

OCEAN, SUN, BOY

ONE AFTERNOON LEAF HELD HIS green hand up to the sky and watched as the rays pierced his fingers until they were translucent.

A shape emerged between him and the sun: a sunspot of a boy rose from the surf. Black skin and tight curly hair bejeweled with sea foam and white bits of sand and shell. Water beaded off his shoulders, and his chest swelled with heavy, patterned breathing.

A filthy white loincloth kept a tentative grip between his legs. His body was compact and muscled; sinewy arms and legs looked like they could shoot from his body like spears. They studied each other. The boy from the sea spoke first and questioned the ponderous green bean before him, seemingly calm but with an alien curiosity awakening within ocher eyes. The dark child of the ocean surveyed the island, taking stock of the dilapidated house, smooth dunes, and dry grass. Satisfied that all was as it appeared to be, benign, no place for pirates or slavers, he dropped his guard and questioned the boy at length. Leaf's answers were quizzical and brief but with enough warmth to invite further conversation. Eventually, both boys sat cross-legged by the pool.

As they talked, Scallop molded the sand into a map of his life: boats, fish, crescent islands. He fished every day with his father. They lived in their boat. If his father was going out to deep waters, he would often drop the boy off at an island to scavenge; if his catch was good, there might not be enough room in the boat for both of them, so sometimes he would retrieve his son late, after taking his catch to market. But Scallop's time was not idle. Deposited on a slip of land, he gathered driftwood and set crab traps. He explained that his father did not take him to the deeper waters because of the slavers who roamed waves in giant boats that could not make shallow water. Many fishermen stuck close to shore, skirting the remaining keys to cast their nets in grassy shallows. Others risked all for bigger fish, the majestic marlin, which could feed a family for over a week.

Scallop gesticulated wildly as he spoke, like a palm tree bending in the storm of his narration. Leaf was stock still, raptly listening, noticing their every difference: the scars that laced Scallop's elbows and knees contrasted with Leaf's smooth, pliable emerald flesh. Leaf's limbs were twig-like, reedy, while the other boy's every movement sprang with articulate muscles. His hands never stopped moving.

Leaf offered to make some of his special tea. Scallop explored the house while Leaf remained in the kitchen to tend the battered brass kettle on the woodstove. He surreptitiously plucked a leaf from his neck and shredded it into the steeping pot. Floorboards groaned as Scallop made his way from room to room.

More sun shone through the warped and rotten kitchen walls than before. Another hurricane and the house would be gone.

As Scallop plodded down the loose stairs, Leaf shook the last of Nanny's tins for anything to eat, but they were all bare.

Scallop repaired the old crab traps and strung them out by the sandbar. Together Leaf and Scallop circled the island and gathered driftwood. Skate shyly followed their progress, a silent silhouette just below the surf. Leaf could tell he was excited and jealous but wanted only to watch first before being introduced.

The boys sat on the shore and waited. The wind picked up, and the clouds gathered their girth as the sun eased westward.

Scallop became quietly anxious and scrutinized the horizon. He spotted his father's boat well before Leaf, and the tension fell from his shoulders. Leaf reclined farther and pulled as much sun into his pores as possible while Scallop rose and dusted the sand from his thighs. Leaf marveled at how pale his palms were compared to the rest of his skin. The lines of his palms cut across his flesh like taut fishing lines, a frenzy of latitude and longitude and courses not yet set. A frown crossed Scallop's face, and he almost spoke. Leaf sensed confusion as if Scallop worried that leaving him alone on the island was akin to abandonment.

"I think it's funny how we say 'sunset,' when really, it's nothing of the kind. It's the world that's turning away from the sun. The light doesn't leave us; we turn away from it. And yet it always comes back."

Scallop nodded, turned to mark his father's progress, and then stepped toward the surf, looking over his shoulder at the green boy reclining among the dunes.

"I think it's okay with you if I keep the crab traps out overnight. I'll be back to check them tomorrow."

The sky bruised a royal purple. Gulls cried.

"That's fine."

Leaf felt sleepy and content.

"See you later."

Scallop trotted toward his father's boat, a bucket of frustrated crabs bouncing in his hand.

Leaf watched him go; he had never seen another boy before. Though he had known that when he did, the other would not be green (Nanny had prepared him for that much), Leaf still assumed that the boy would be his twin in every other regard. He felt the thought foolish. After all, Skate was flat, mischievous, and altogether different. But Leaf knew that he and Skate were the exceptions and expected similarities, not differences. Leaf never dreamed, but as his eyes closed, he imagined that the rich darkness that enveloped him belonged to Scallop, that the dark boy from the ocean cast a germinating shadow that demanded Leaf flower wildly through the night.

SKATE AND SCALLOP TOOK TO each other instantly. Scallop could hold his breath underwater for an exceptionally long time. They could fish together and quickly became an adept team; Skate would flush out flounder or drive a school of silver fish toward Scallop's waiting spear or net. This constant bounty meant that Scallop's father left him more and more on the island.

The lengthy network of sandbars that kept most boats away was a natural breeding ground for crab and many kinds of fish. They hung the sail across the pool to collect the morning dew and rainfall. Several of Nanny's tomato plants thrived again with a regular water source. Scallop would emerge from the surf, drop his catch into a bucket and drink from the cool water gathered within the sail and placed in the shade of the house, or have tea with his lunch of tomato and crab. He would snap off a sprig of aloe and squeeze its lime-colored jelly onto his skin to treat any scrapes or cuts.

One afternoon, while Leaf sunned by the pool, Scallop called out from the shore, sounding confused and scared. Leaf ran to the beach. Skate roiled the water with concern. Scallop stood on the sand, ankles smeared with seaweed, holding his arm.

"We had this sea bass cornered, a real fat bastard, perfect dinner, tons of urchins around though, no big deal, be careful, careful—"

He sputtered and coughed up a bit of water.

A look of concern deepened across Leaf's brow as Scallop displayed his inner arm. A small wound leaked blood diluted from the water coursing off his skin.

"And a lionfish came out of nowhere. I mean, I must have startled it. It sure startled me! Skate scooted backward, I nearly did a back flip underwater, and that's when I got stuck."

He was shaking so severely that Leaf eased him down onto the sand.

"I—I just don't know what struck me. The fish or one of the urchins."

Scallop's knees dug deeper into the sand. He held his injured arm and desperately looked out to sea for his father's boat.

Skate writhed in the surf, rippling his body to deliver a message Leaf had nearly guessed: the lionfish, a winged creature with barbed fins, was poisonous. Deadly. Scallop's chest heaved as his heart beat rapidly. They locked eyes. His pupils flashed a wildness Leaf had never before imagined. A vulnerable hunger had risen to the surface. The proud yet wounded boy sensed that his new friend had caught sight of the fearsome sea-wolf within, which clawed up through the foam of his corneas and quickly turned his head. Leaf pulled him up and led him by the hand to the shade of the house. Scallop gulped air as tears gathered at the corner of his eyes. Leaf left him reclining in the lawn chair as he rushed to the kitchen. He pulled all of the leaves from around his neck as the stove warmed. The soft spines of the aloe plant massing at the empty window pane languidly reached for the sun. From outside, he could hear stifled sobs. Leaf begged the rainwater to boil and nearly spilled the tea as he rushed to his friend's side. He squatted beside him as Scallop drank deeply and gasped as the powerful tonic surged throughout his body.

Leaf took Nanny's shark tooth from around his neck and cut his finger. Dark green blood beaded. Scallop, wide-eyed, teethed on the chipped and dirty teacup. His breathing had decelerated.

Leaf touched the puncture on Scallop's arm and felt fluid pulse from his cut and into the injury. Scallop's eyelids fluttered, then closed. He straightened his legs as his other arm went slack. Leaf concentrated on the sunlight coating the top of his skull and channeled that energy through his finger. And into Scallop. Leaf relaxed, a conduit of light, as the other boy twitched and stiffened.

One leg shot out. A rise in Scallop's crotch stretched the tight confines of his loincloth. Lips parted as his body calmed. Leaf lifted his finger from the wound; the flesh there was new and white. His own cut had closed, only a pale green line, lighter than the rest of his skin but fading.

Scallop blinked and smiled weakly. He lifted the cup of tea for another sip. He stared at Leaf with bewildered gratitude and noticed the ragged tear of missing petals from around his throat. He let the tea in his mouth dribble back into the cup. Alert now, Scallop covered his lap with both hands and looked over his shoulder, out at the ocean braided by the chop of distant waves.

"Thank you, Leaf. I don't know what to say; I just can't believe I have been...."

He looked at the lukewarm, sea-green water in the cup. "I can't believe I have been drinking you all this time."

Leaf gripped his knees and rocked back on his heels. "I have always made my own tea."

"Well, you saved me. I just—"

"We don't know if the poison was in you or if it was just a puncture from an urchin. What matters is that you're fine now."

Scallop narrowed his eyes and nodded. He saw Leaf differently. No judgment crossed his face, though. Nor shame. He moved his hands from his lap and spread his legs. The stiffness there had subsided. He seemed to ponder something but jumped up and stretched, then marveled at the white spot on his arm.

"We should go tell Skate I'm okay. He was really worried."

Leaf followed him to the shore, the sun on his back a reassuring push in the right direction.

LUNAR
BRIDGES

SCALLOP INVITED LEAF TO LAST Bridge. He and his father went once a month or so. Leaf said yes, but had reservations. The idea of being on a boat frightened him. The prospect of falling overboard or the boat sinking meant death. Yet to be far from land, all that reflected sunlight pitching off the waves had an allure. He had never seen a city, even a fractured one like Last Bridge.

As hurricanes pulled the Keys apart, certain spans of bridge remained. Romanesque stretches of ruined asphalt made for stable squatting. Tiny cities rose. Rippled plywood casinos, thatch bordellos, and tarpaulin schoolhouses crowded these stretches; myriad fishing lines trolled the placid waters below. Last Bridge throbbed and tottered across the longest stretch of bridge still standing among the withered Florida Keys. Landless at both broken ends, it stretched toward nothingness like a doomed and smoky dream—a small city precariously balanced on its back as if a gigantic spine was knobbed and knotted with calcified tumors infested with raucous vermin.

Leaf barely fit into the boat. Scallop sat at the bow, perched patiently like an expectant heron. Leaf huddled in the middle, surrounded by bundles of fish. Their gasping eyes must have imagined that the sky was the sea, distant yet attainable. A few flopped about, but as they sailed south, all became still. Scallop's father spoke little. He was an older, perfectly somber version of Scallop. Their bodies were nearly identical, though the father was more defined, his musculature carved deeper into his body but still elastic. Every aspect of the boat was an extension of him.

His face was heavily lined from permanently squinting against the blazing sun. His cheeks were a mass of black moles. Scallop's were still clear.

Skate didn't show the morning of their departure and had been aloof the previous day. Though he'd fast taken to Scallop, Leaf worried that his first friend was jealous.

While Scallop's father expertly controlled the skiff, Leaf turned back and forth between the two and studied their similarities.

Though the father was slightly smaller and more compact, he did not seem diminished; where Scallop was an observer, his father was contemplative action; the boy was learning the craft, and the father was the craft. Though the man rarely spoke, Leaf sensed an internal compass and recognized that ultimately he had more in common with the father than his son. He rode the waves and, by extension, the sea. Leaf was a silent sun sailor. Both had an axis, something that Scallop longed for. Leaf felt ocean spray on his face for the first time as the boat broke over the waves. As they sailed along, he also felt, for the first time, the explicit wind of a chosen direction.

LAST BRIDGE WAS A MASSIVE arc of taut fishing lines and tiny rolling boats. A cascade of naked children tumbled and hooted into the water off one side while an entire community relieved itself from the other. Knowingly, Scallop's father approached from the correct flank. The size of the pocked, cracked cement pillars impressed Leaf. At once, he understood Nanny's wistful longing for the shattered cities: if this broken highway stood sentinel for the lost lunar landscapes of the past, what must the broken towers and bombed palaces have been like?

They anchored beneath a worn rope ladder and loaded a net with fish and a large orange conch. Scallop's father went first, scurrying up the rope as fast as any of the feral bridge children. A drop of his sweat spiraled down and hit Leaf's forehead like pungent rain as he swiftly pulled their cargo up, and he was gone without a word to his son. The boys were free to roam the dirty avenue.

This artificial island was a strange dish. Scallop adopted the stance of an urban veteran and pretended nonchalance while Leaf gaped. Music flowed out of a silver box hoisted on the shoulder of a wizened, blind, dreadlocked oldster with one leg.

Giant starfish pulsed alternating colors in rusty buckets. Families crowded into one another like mammalian anemones, all tugging hands, and crying mouths. It appeared as if everyone on Last Bridge bred constantly and contemptuously, daring the sea not to pull down their battered boats by filling them with weeping red babies. Leaf was shocked by the sheer number of people and struggled for a reference point. The best he could come up with was that they seemed like spiteful cattails bending under an invisible wind, rushing from each other only to be whipped back again. He smelled a strange, unfamiliar smoke, alluring and distasteful.

He looked to Scallop for guidance.

"Marijuana," he knowingly sniffed.

The green boy tilted his head while Scallop rolled his eyes. The pungent odor made him queasy—the thought of burning fresh plant matter revolted Leaf. The driftwood he burned for Nanny's tea was dried and dead, but this was different; this smelled like a delirious scream.

The center of the road was crowded, forcing people to touch as they passed. Leaf smelled sweat and the oils meant to disguise sweat. No one paid any attention to the color of his skin. A young, pretty girl with a single, curious eye in the middle of her forehead whistled past. An old man burned by decades beneath the sun into a dark collection of cancerous moles, his exposed back a labyrinth of floppy polyps, fished over the side; armless, he lazily let out the line from his fishing pole with long, dexterous toes. Scallop paused.

"Put your hand on my shoulder, so we don't get separated."

The crowd thickened. Elbows jarred their ribs, fishing poles swung before Leaf's face, children stepped on his toes. They came upon a giant, ragged hole in the middle of the bridge and the crowd flowed naturally around it. The asphalt bent toward a sudden shock of calm blue water, revealing that this dirty ribbon of humanity was a rare and lonely strand suspended over an immense and unsympathetic ocean. Leaf looked up to the clean sun for a burst of reassurance. A small naked boy, head a mass of wiry blond hair, gingerly approached the edge of the hole, turned, squatted, and defecated. He quickly rose and was swallowed by the crowd.

Scallop had brought a metal basket of the better crabs to trade. As the bridge began a slow incline, he led Leaf toward its ragged end. The shops and shacks ceased; long plywood casinos filled with sad men and bored women pushed to the edge of the bridge. Bordellos stretched under colorful canvas, weathered from the inside by yellowing smoke. Patches of pavement were smeared with bird shit and trampled human feces, fish bones, and the black stains of countless cooking fires. A naked woman with painted breasts parted the beggars and alarmed chickens to gather flapping laundry from a line of sheets and worn sarongs.

Beggars inched toward the boys with hands out, toothless mouths open. Some were missing eyes, some limbs. Having never been in a crowd, Leaf smiled at the beggars and examined them, wondering who had taken their limbs and what aspects of life wore away eyes and teeth. He was just about to ask Scallop, who had intervened and pushed a few away with his foot, when his friend announced, "We are here to see the Flamingo."

A few of the beggars recoiled; those deaf or insane kept at them. Leaf's hand slipped from Scallop's shoulder as he tilted his head quizzically.

"The White Flamingo is a fortune teller, but she also owns one of these casinos and runs the bordellos. This end of the bridge is hers."

A large pelican regarded them with suspicion from atop a pole.

Leaf stared back at the bird. He had seen countless pelicans before, but this one seemed different: its eyes were human, malicious, and watchful. As Scallop led Leaf to a small hut cobbled together from sheets of plywood and corrugated metal, the bird spread its white wings and dove off the pole to glide over the waves.

Scallop whispered, "The White Flamingo is an albino. Her allergy to the sun is extreme: her skin cankers and erupts into little feathers when exposed to daylight. She avoids the sun at all costs, though she's had enough past exposure that her skull is stitched with white feathers instead of hair."

A beautiful, bare-chested young girl emerged from the hut and smiled. Her skin was as white as a sand dollar bleached by the sun. She held a curtain back for them to enter. A pale boy, obviously her twin, stepped forward and relieved Scallop of the crabs as powerful incense overwhelmed them. Leaf hovered near the entrance, concerned that he would swoon in the abrupt darkness.

Overpowering scents kept him alert: dusty perfumes and stale marijuana. Scallop was swallowed by the darkness. Until his eyes adjusted, all Leaf could see of him were his glistening shoulder blades, as if he were a corpse bobbing facedown in a black ocean.

The albino children lit candles. In a corner, the White Flamingo reclined on a colorful pile of tattered silk pillows. Glass beads poured from the ceiling and hung at various lengths, robbing the room of any sense of perspective. Leaf wavered. The White Flamingo snapped her fingers and pointed at the curtain. The girl bowed and secured the flap, so it hung open just enough to feed Leaf sunlight while still blanketing the seer in shadow.

She was a tall woman, gangly, all limb, appropriately birdlike, with a weak chin and hooked nose. Her large brow erupted in white feathers. Some effort had been made to comb them back, but several resisted, giving her the appearance of having just flown through a storm. Smaller feathers grasped her scalp but could not conceal elongated earlobes that, stressed from the weight of preposterous earrings, brushed her shoulders. She wore a sleeveless white shirt cut high above her midriff, exposing a few scars that bled feathers. A giant diamond slept in the ovoid of her belly button. A weather-beaten Ouija board obscured her lap. Her useless hands lay on the board, palms up. Repeated sun exposure had scarred them into white claws. A semblance of nails twisted up out of the mass of feathers.

Scallop somberly knelt before her. Again Leaf was surprised by how light the soles of his feet were; even dirty, they seemed translucent. He tried to read some meaning from the dark hieroglyphs etched into each foot.

The White Flamingo spoke. Her voice was chirpy yet relaxed.

"Thank you for your offering."

Scallop shifted, so he was now on both knees.

"This is Leaf."

Leaf didn't know what to do, so he bowed and squatted beside Scallop. "I am so glad you finally have a friend. Please, have a drink."

Scallop's cheeks darkened, but he seemed pleased. The albino children brought small coconut shells, halved and hollowed, filled with a clear liquid. Scallop drained the coconut bowl, eyes solemnly closed, in several large gulps. Leaf tested his: surprisingly cool rainwater. Yet he sensed a plant extract, gustless but potent. He drank deeply and looked at Scallop.

Beads of water clung to his parted lips. His teeth seemed eager and sharp in the darkness. The children took their cups while the White Flamingo shook her useless hands and looked up into the galaxy of glass beads above. Leaf followed her gaze: the beads began to sway slightly. Light danced within. Warmth tickled his skin. He hadn't noticed that several strands looped between the hollow eyes of petite bird skulls. Scallop sighed. Whatever the rainwater was laced with, it was having an effect. The White Flamingo leaned forward and clutched Leaf's chin with a feathered claw. She held Scallop's face in her other hand; he was wide-eyed and stared at her in complete awe. As she stroked his cheek, the beads above twinkled, then dimmed.

The bird skulls silently chuckled.

"I am sorry, Scallop, but you will not catch the fish you seek."

And she looked truly sad, her white skin even more ashen; her large eyes teared. As she turned to Leaf, he felt her eyes filling with octopus ink.

"You. You will reach for the sun while staying rooted to the ground." She peered into him, and the ink in her eyes suddenly curdled with dread.

"But I fear your shadow will be much too long." She whispered this last prophecy, shuddered, and fell back into a valley of pillows. One of the twins quickly wrapped her in a shawl while the other held the curtain back and swept an arm outward, inviting an exit.

THE BOYS STEPPED INTO SUDDEN sunlight. Everything was brighter, sharper. From behind the curtain, they heard the twins consoling the White Flamingo as she wept over their fortunes. Scallop kicked at a dehydrated crab, a likely escapee from a previous supplicant's offerings.

"I don't know what she meant about you, Leaf. But just remember what she said."

He picked up the crab and held it at arm's length. It slowly opened and closed its free pincher, grasping nothing but air.

"But I've always wanted to fish for shark. Shark fins fetch a lot of jump on Marathon Key. People think shark-fin soup cures all kinds of ailments. I think she was telling me not to go after sharks. Yes, a bad business for me."

He looked disappointed but resolved as he walked over to the concrete railing. Leaf was silent. The sun boring into the top of his head reassured him, though he still felt numbed by the mysterious rainwater, the cloudy prophecy. He craved the solitude of his private island and was beginning to understand that the repellant and attractive aspects of humanity were closely intertwined.

"But I am great with the net. Nobody in the Keys can crab like me," Scallop continued to himself. He dropped the crab over the railing. He forced a smile and flicked his gaze back toward the White Flamingo's tent.

"And don't worry about her. She cries over everyone's future."

Unseen by the boys, before the tumbling crab could reach the safety of water, the massive pelican from before swooped down and caught it in the basket of its bill.

SCALLOP'S FATHER STEERED THEM HOME. He was pleasantly drunk and turned the tiller over to his son. The sail flagged, and Scallop worried they would have to row back or tack endlessly, but it soon filled with wind, and they were on their way. During the fallow period, his father leaned over the bow and vomited. Scallop looked out to sea while Leaf marveled at the number of small fish that streamed out of nowhere to peck greedily at the red chunks of alcohol-infused fruit bobbing in the water. Scallop's father laughed and combed the water with his fingers, mouth open in a foolish grin. Leaf had not yet seen Scallop's father anything other than focused, and it was strange to hear him talk about anything other than fishing as if he had no other thoughts or desires. He had visited a brothel and the casinos. The lines around his eyes were still deep but relaxed. His wrinkles were ripples on the ocean rather than the lines of a net pulled until frayed.

The wind picked up, and they were off. Scallop urged the skiff forward to get his friend home before sundown. The giant pelican followed. Once the island was sighted, the bird banked northward. Instead of the typical talons of a sea bird, a solitary human hand hung below its midriff. It bore a gold ring of amethyst on one finger that sparkled in contrast to the unambiguous black conviction that filled its eyes.

HURRICANE

THE SKY WAS CLOUDLESS—A wonderful, guileless blue. Skate glided beside Leaf as he walked the beach. He forcefully regurgitated a shell of particular beauty, launching it perfectly into Leaf's cupped hands: a glossy cat's eye, an empty swirl of knowledge.

Scallop had announced that he and his father would be away fishing for several days. When they parted, he put his hands on Leaf's slim shoulders as he said goodbye, reminding him of things he knew to do: secure the crab traps, water the plants—mindless advice that allowed them to lock eyes for longer than necessary. Scallop measured his reflection within the depth of flecked amber that cleaved Leaf's pupils. Leaf forded the pitch of Scallop's orbs and dove deep, looking for his own heart. As usual, Skate was good company. As he provided shells, Leaf deposited them faithfully around the empty pool like a prehistoric parade of spindly artifacts, a frozen arboretum of coral and sea-polished bone.

Leaf hauled driftwood up to the house out of habit, to have handy for

Scallop to repair crab traps or for the stove if he ever wanted a cup of tea again (he'd passed since the incident with the lionfish). Tomatoes bloomed in a bucket of dirt beside the back door. After piling the driftwood, Leaf knelt to examine the dusty, sun-baked soil; rainwater had ignited some errant seeds, tomato, and vine looped within the bucket. On a whim, Leaf decided to experiment and bent one of his fingers backward. It refused to give, so he went into the kitchen for a knife. He placed the finger on the counter and started cutting just above the top joint. It gave easily, like a carrot. He felt no pain. A pulpy fluid fanned out across the counter's surface. He held his hand aloft. A few drops wound down his wrist, and the bleeding stopped. The wound exposed vegetable flesh packed around a robust reed of bone, the mouth closed as emerald blood coagulated and stiffened into sticky molasses.

Outside, he carefully planted the severed fingertip in a bucket that contained a fledging vine of tomatoes, so it was sticking straight up as if it were trying to note which direction the wind was blowing. He walked around the pool until he found a large scallop shell half-full with evaporating rainwater. He poured the water over his planted finger and patted the soil down, so it had a firm mooring. He then ambled over to the beach to see if Skate had found any shells of interest.

※

IN THE MORNING, LEAF TESTED the lines of the traps. Some were quite heavy with crab. Scallop would be delighted when he returned.

Leaf scanned the horizon but did not see any sign of his friend, though the black smoke of a giant slaver ship marred the sky. He examined his fingertip: it had re-grown during the night.

The skin was the maturing color of a green banana about to go yellow. There was a slight circular ridge where it had emerged from the wound and nearly filled out to its original size.

He spent the afternoon absorbing sun by the pool. Errant gulls lurked overhead. He moved around in his chair occasionally to keep the noxious birds from roosting on his body. In the late afternoon, he checked on his finger plant. It had grown: a newly formed joint pushed through the dirt, extending the finger by half an inch, and in doing so, the finger plant had turned and now appeared as if it were beckoning someone to follow.

The following day when he awoke, Scallop was standing over him, hands on his hips, laughing.

"Man, I was going to say it's not natural to sleep like that, but then again, you're nothing but all-natural, right?"

He extended his hand to help Leaf up. His warm calluses felt like small, private suns massaging the flesh of his friend's green hand. Rivulets of sweat and seawater snaked off his body. They walked toward the shore and stopped at the water's edge. The newborn sky was still devouring gray-black clouds.

Bouncing on his heels, Scallop asked, "Notice anything new?"

Eyebrows arched in mock amusement, Scallop tilted his head toward the ocean. A skiff rocked gently in the surf. Confusion flashed across Leaf's face.

"That's my boat, silly. I've got my own boat now." He slapped his chest and put one foot in the water as if he were now master of land and sea.

"I think Flamingo told my dad it was time for me to have a boat. And this means he can fish deeper waters now and wants me to set more crab traps around your island from now on." He nodded, admiring the boat, surveying the ocean, and measuring possibilities. He talked about his plans to set more crab traps, the fish he and his father could net, saving enough jump for a bigger boat.... Leaf knew he was trying not to think about one thing, the elusive shark that the White Flamingo had warned about, looming somewhere in the murky channels of the future.

⚘

LEAF SAT BESIDE THE POOL. The sun sparkled; sunspots erupted.

The pores of his green flesh dilated to swallow every morsel of light. Across such an enormous distance, the eruptions felt like dragonflies brushing against his eyelashes. Scallop joined him, gulping rainwater while he ate several oranges and a sandwich of fried fish and hard bread left over from the trip to Last Bridge. He ate silently and fast and then rushed back to his boat.

After he left, Leaf scooped up the orange rinds to use as compost and went behind the house to inspect the finger plant. He was surprised to discover that an entire hand had broken through the soil. It looked as if it were slowly reaching for the nearest tomato. Leaf compared his own hand to the one growing in the bucket. The planted hand was smaller but otherwise the same.

He shredded the orange peel, pushed it into the soil, and watered the hand before sauntering back to the vacant pool.

The following day he checked on the plant hand again. Leaf was shocked to see that it had multiplied overnight. Several hands had emerged of varying sizes from the same thick, leafy wrist. And each one clutched a frightened tomato. The tomato plant was nearly consumed by the hand bush, their stalks interchangeable; the original finger cutting must have grafted itself onto the root of the tomato plant. Leaf retrieved some morning dew and cautiously watered the hand plant. Shifting some plywood so that it would not be easily seen from the pool, he went to find Skate.

SUN ON HIS SHOULDERS, HE squatted by the lapping waves and waited for Skate to make an appearance—in the distance, two small boats appeared. Scallop's new craft cut the waves while his father sped toward darker water at full sail. Scallop beached his boat and waded back out to check some traps as Skate shot out of the water and then harried his ankles. When Scallop made shore, he and Leaf skipped shells with Skate, who rushed to catch them and spit them back. In the afternoon, Scallop used one of Nanny's old sheets to make a breezy tent in the sand beside Leaf's lawn chair. After lunch, he dozed while his green friend basked in the bright, cloudless noon. He spent the rest of the day pulling in crab traps and spearing fish. Much later, he waited patiently on the shore for his father to return. As the sun began to set, Scallop did not move. Arms crossed over his knees, he monitored the distant surf, his head bobbing with the waves' rhythm. Specks of sand clung to his eyebrows like errant stars at the fringe of a distant galaxy. His lips were dry and cracked. Leaf joined him, and together, they watched the choppy tide. As the earth rolled away from the sun, eddies of darkness lulled Leaf toward sleep. For the first time in his life, he fought slumber and craved nighttime consciousness.

The forlorn cry of gulls ceased as the birds nestled down into the dunes for the night. Even the waves seemed to subside.

As Leaf's eyes closed for the last time, he saw Scallop's face harden: this night would be his darkest, longest, loneliest.

Leaf struggled against that last fate but was doomed as the last of the light withdrew from the weary world.

THE FIRST RAYS OF DAWN massaged Leaf's thigh and leg. He turned to let
the sunlight stroke his full form and paint his lips and cheeks. Sand fleas
scurried in every direction as he brushed off the sand that dotted his legs.
Scallop was asleep beside him.

Moist clumps of sand were pasted to his dark skin; he had pulled
his knees up to his chest in a fetal ball of frustration. A line of seaweed
grasped their ankles where the high tide had nearly reached to claim them
for the ocean. Either of them could have easily been pulled out to sea.
Leaf reflexively kicked himself back from the water's edge. Scallop's face
was half-hidden by his arms—a compressed mollusk of deep pain. Leaf
scurried over the dunes toward the house to brew some tea for his friend,
wounded again, pierced by something less tangible but more deadly.

The injury was to his heart.

As he crossed the sand-snaked cracked concrete surrounding the
pool, Leaf noticed that the piece of plywood he had used to conceal the
hand-plant had been pushed aside. The bucket of soil had been upended
and dragged several feet. It was ruptured and empty, its black dirt poured
across the white sand like granulated entrails. A path of eviscerated
tomatoes smeared toward the dunes. Leaf followed the trail of pulpy
vegetable matter and dirt over the small hills of sand. A fury of large
palm prints pinwheeled toward the ocean, right to the water's edge. The
fingerprints were three times the size of Leaf's. He returned to the house,
righted the bucket, and swept the trail away with a palm frond.

As the water boiled on the stove in the kitchen, he tore a white petal
from around his neck. Leaf rubbed it between his fingers as it lightly
browned and curled along the edge of the tear. The kettle rumbled as
he ripped the petal into bits and ground it in the bottom of a dusty bowl
with his green thumb. The kettle whistled, and Leaf knew that Scallop
would wave it away and refuse any sustenance or comfort until his father

returned. He also knew that, for the first time, he had brewed a cup of tea for himself.

ON THE BEACH, SCALLOP REMAINED stoically vigilant. He held his fishing spear and stood so still that a heron landed and moved close, sorting the clumps of seaweed with its bill for anything edible. Spooked when it realized Scallop was a living being, it took flight. Intuiting that his friend did not want to talk but would not be bothered by his presence, Leaf sat beside him. Midmorning, black tentacles of smoke from an unseen slave ship poisoned the sky, anointing their unspoken fear: Scallop's father had been taken. It was also possible that he had gone out too far and been stuck in some luckless patch of ocean without wind. Adrift, his boat could flounder for days. But his father knew water and wind as if the sail were an extension of his soul. Skate flummoxed as close to shore as he could, desperate to comfort his friend.

At high tide, they spotted the empty husk of a boat.

Scallop saw it first, moaned, and trotted listlessly into the water. He dove and swam to the black speck bobbing beyond the sandbar. When he reached the craft, he lay down in the bow on his stomach and paddled toward shore. Leaf waded out to meet him, fighting off the narcotic effect of diffused sunlight lapping around his ankles. He felt unsteady as Skate nervously nudged him along. As Scallop neared, Leaf saw that the boat's frame was uneven, charred. It had been burned to the waterline, its sail and tiller gone. Scallop's father had been taken by slavers. The fearful rumors that swirled around the slavers were their armor and best weapon. The captured were sold as slaves or pressed to become pirates in the slave trade themselves. Women and infants were cooked and eaten. Slavers wore festive necklaces of their victims' painted teeth.

Scallop rolled off the scarred hulk and submerged himself underwater.

He rose and dove, rose and dove, a strange, manic maneuver. With each plunge, he would rise, water pouring off his head, mouth opened in a silent scream, an attempt to purge tears that would never stop. Leaf, shaken and weak from his exposure to the water, was forced to return to shore. Skate mournfully knocked his head on the hull of the ruined craft and then sped away. The black smoke on the horizon dissipated. The cry of an unseen gull mocked the boys, one on the beach, immobile, tears running down his cheeks. At the same time, the other built a ritual of submersion and thrust as if he were a spear plunging into pain itself, but with every stab and leap, cold water rushed to fill the void his body made, the froth of his actions a salty scar absorbed by the ocean.

LEAF SAT, CROSS-LEGGED AND LISTLESS beneath the sun, as Scallop pulled the crab traps past him and around to the pool to the back of the house. He laid the nets out to dry on the sand. He was making preparations to leave. Leaf called Scallop's name, but he was lost in thought, lips moving silently, every muscle articulate and strained. Finally, Leaf touched his wrist as he passed and jumped, startled. The muscles in his neck seemed twisted and wrong, but his eyes were cold and clear.

"I want to come with you."

Scallop exhaled and looked down. Sand sparkled on his knuckles.

His breathing slowed, and his mouth unknotted. A look of disappointment darkened his face. Leaf drew his knees to his chest and thought, He doesn't want me along. But Scallop grabbed his hand and squeezed it, and Leaf understood that Scallop was not concerned that he would be a burden but that he might witness failure; slavers were ephemeral sharks, ghostly hunters that everyone avoided and no one tried to catch. Two boys with fishing spears and a human manta ray were about to try.

LEAF HELPED SCALLOP PACK THE boat. Skate excitedly fluttered about the bow. They piled provisions into the skiff, stuff they needed to survive, and items from the house to barter or trade. High tide came early and claimed more beach than usual.

As Leaf exited the house for the last time, he noticed that it bent toward the ocean more than before, as if it were exhausted, ready to surrender to the next hurricane. He wondered if he would have a home to return to.

Scallop pushed the boat off the shore, clumps of sand spinning from behind his heels. Leaf watched the island recede.

Cattails furiously waved goodbye in the wind. Once the skiff reached open water, Skate rode the wake rolling off the bow. Scallop squatted by the tiller, the rope from the sail loose in one hand. The pain from his face had withdrawn to his eyes, which were quiet and intent on pulling an intangible truth from somewhere just beyond the horizon. Leaf absently plucked at one of the petals around his neck and thought of the growing, disembodied clump of hands blindly clawing its way across the ocean floor. He shuddered to think that a part of him had been set loose and was out of his control. He let go of the petal, lest he accidentally pull it out and the wind takes it.

The boat tacked. They headed north, though first, they would stop at Marathon Key, the only city of significance in the Keys besides Last Bridge. They were half a day away. Beyond that was their unspoken goal:

Canal City, the fractured, half-sunken remains of mean Miami, ruled by the ruthless King Pelicans.

Its inventors were among the first to wield the genie box wand. The boxes were more potent and less erratic during those early war years, and their creators were as crafty in their use as design. Their recast avian forms possessed the only brainpan large enough to contain the human mind. Replacing talons with a single hand to continue their malicious use of twisted technologies, they roosted within the ruins and exerted control far beyond their twisted wingspan. For the boys, success meant not only finding Scallop's father but evading omnipresent avian eyes.

CROCODILE
EYES

THE WATER SURROUNDING MARATHON Key was filled with refuse. The air was tinged with the scent of burning meat and garbage.

Salts have a saying: You can smell Marathon before you see it.

And before they sighted land, the boys saw the vast undulating halo of seagulls which dove and flapped in continual cries of hunger above the docks and fishing vessels. Scallop tacked and slowed. He tried to determine the best approach. There was no welcoming point of entry as Marathon was all port and continuous dock. Dingy houseboats rocked as naked children dove off their bows to relieve themselves in the very water that fisherman on the rickety piers drew their catch from. Out at sea, the silhouette of a monstrous tanker lurked in the distance. Slavers— their presence a reminder that the island's Coast Guard, a band of sailors serving the only boat with a working engine, not under pirate command, was the only recognized authority in the Keys.

But their jurisdiction ended when Marathon was no longer in sight.

When slave ships lingered, fishermen brought the Coast Guard more than their usual share of the day's catch.

Skate came up to the bow, his whole being boiling with questions.

The beaches were too choked with people and shanties for a proper landing. Scallop jumped overboard with the anchor.

Surfacing, he pushed away a floating chain of feces and asked Skate to guard the boat. He launched into a leisurely backstroke toward shore, calling out to Leaf.

"Come on, I'll keep an eye on you."

Leaf hesitated.

"Don't worry, I'll be with you. Come on, I need you."

Scallop paused and dog-paddled to keep his head above water.

Leaf had never heard Scallop say he needed anything before. This crack in his friend's self-sufficiency shook Leaf from his stupor, and he wrinkled his nose and slid into the water.

And felt light wafting up. Mercurial strands of sunlight filtered through the water and tickled Leaf's feet and caressed his thighs. He nearly languished; it felt so good, golden, and right. Leaf wanted to just float away, but Scallop pulled on his wrist. His touch sparked a thought: Maybe I have been afloat my entire life. Leaf tried to focus. Aiming for shore, he pushed forward with a strong kick and momentarily passed Scallop, who looked surprised and pleased and easily matched his pace.

The surface of the water was a mat of waste, dead fish, broken net, and coarse seaweed. They pushed through until a fishing line caught the corner of Leaf's mouth. As he struggled to untangle himself, a black mass of decaying plastic wrapped around his head. Blinded, already unsure of being in the water, Leaf reeled and kicked madly. Scallop supported him with a calm hand under his arm while he methodically removed the debris. Leaf went limp. Closer to shore, the sunlight hardly penetrated the polluted water, so Leaf felt less drunk from refraction though he was still sluggish. Scallop sensed this, and once the trash was clear, he hooked his arm under Leaf's chin and frog-kicked toward the dirty beach. Leaf saw blue sky occasionally streaked by black dragons of smoke. The sun painted his cheeks and brow. Leaf felt life return, flowing all the way to his toes. He gave a weak kick to help Scallop and let him know he was well. The corner of his mouth felt raw. He thought of how filthy the water was and strained to keep his head elevated. And then rough, uneven land was beneath their feet. Shells and debris dug at their heels.

They stood in the churning surf, turned, and faced the thriving Marathon Key wreckage.

Leaf stepped back but was pushed forward by a large wave. Marathon was nothing like Last Bridge. Marathon was land. Standing on the shore, he could not see where the beach ended, nor could he fathom the shape or scope of the island.

Vertigo struck. And everywhere, people. A haphazard boardwalk hung over the surf. A pile of people slumbered in the shade beneath. Naked children sorted trash while above men burned black by the sun fished, side by side with wild-haired women cradling infants or bottles of rum or both. Youths in dirty shorts squatted by the shore and rolled joints, their long hair flames of different colors. They coolly observed the boys, white eyes looking out from greasy black and white paint masks.

Scallop looked at Leaf, concerned. Leaf clutched the petals at his neck and nodded reassuringly to signal that he was up to the crowd. And an actual city—just the number of people shocked him. Scallop carefully put a thumb to Leaf's lips and pressed the corner of his mouth.

"You're hurt."

He pulled his thumb away and marveled at the green ooze that glazed its tip.

"It's okay. I heal fast."

Scallop's eye's flashed wide.

"Great White! You're not kidding. The wound's closing as I watch. It was a pretty deep cut."

Leaf closed his eyes and turned toward the sun. The din of the island's populace ceased. Light healed and soothed. The sky was cloudless, and the breeze stopped. His arms dropped to his sides, and he felt as if he were about to levitate, but the sound of humanity returned; the wind resumed. He slowly opened his eyes and smiled at Scallop, who whistled, incredulous and impressed.

"You'll do fine here. Just stick close."

They turned toward the boardwalk. Scallop discreetly sucked the green viscous residue from his thumb. Leaf noticed but didn't say anything, though he couldn't help but wonder, How do I taste?

They scaled a pile of trash-strewn rocks, strolled on the boardwalk, and everywhere there were people. It was as crowded as Last Bridge, but already Leaf noted differences and understood that Last Bridge was more a fishing village, a place of permanent respite, while Marathon throbbed with commerce and the successes and failures that came with it. Scallop pushed through the throng, momentarily abandoning Leaf among feral strangers. A girl with colorful bird wings for ears, like those of a parrot, smiled at him. And then, just as suddenly, Scallop was back, another green boy in tow.

Another green boy. Leaf's jaw dropped. They both stood and stared at each other. At first, Leaf felt like he was looking into a healthier mirror. But even though the other was completely green, where Leaf's cranium was covered with the slightest clover, his was pasted with dirty curls of blonde hair. And he had the muscular definition of someone who knew and used his body, while Leaf was demure and weedy. This other emerald lad had a form that expanded and contracted in the same manner as

Scallop's swimmer's build but was more exaggerated. Patches of his skin were much darker, broken like tectonic plates; they clung to him like bark at his knees, elbows, and across his shoulders.

He smiled an impossible smile, a clip of perfect white bullets, and Leaf shot back a hopeful grin. They shook hands; his strong, callused palms swallowed Leaf's lithe grip. Leaf's eyes traced the surging veins that wired the back of the hand and looped around the forearm to disappear within the pinch of the other boy's armpit.

"Do you live alone on an island, too?" Leaf said with wonder.

The other green boy's grip slackened as he looked toward Scallop.

Scallop gave a curt nod of approval.

"Uh, no. Born and bred on Marathon, Mum drank herself to death. Never knew my dad. I heard he went into the Kudzu Army when I was just a kid." He quickly dropped Leaf's hand and scanned the crowd. Scallop put his hands on both of their shoulders.

"Hardy, this is Leaf, the boy I told you about."

Hardy snapped back to attention. His green eyes, flecked dark brown, focused again on Leaf.

"Ah-ha. You're the guy who never eats? Never had buttered gator tail, not once?"

Leaf shook his head in the affirmative. Hardy retook his hand and flipped it over to examine the other boy's golden palm.

He tugged gently at one of the petals that ringed his neck, but Scallop swatted his hand away with a mirthless laugh.

"Hardy, if you could, I think you'd put him on a scale like a fish."

Hardy laughed. They walked down the middle of the street, arms across one another's shoulders to keep the crowd from dividing them. Scallop and Hardy launched into a rapid, colorful form of speech. They stopped when Leaf looked perplexed.

Scallop slid out from under Hardy's arm and positioned himself beside Leaf. "Marathon, Leafy. It's how people talk here."

Hardy's rutted palm massaged Leaf's shoulder as they explained island argot and the various handshakes and accompanying gestures. Scallop explained their situation to Hardy and enlisted his help. He quickly agreed, and Scallop's face lost some of its pain. They meandered down a twisting sandy path littered with people selling all sorts of wares and food. Colorful clapboard stalls lined the street. Cooking smoke and steam rose from open-air kitchens jammed with benches and barefoot customers dunking raw chunks of bread into fish and kelp soup, washing it down with coconut-flavored rum. Behind these shacks were the remnants of older buildings, the simple hotels and businesses that had defined the island before the Red War.

Now bullet-pocked, each building was challenged by countless repairs, additional floors, wooden structures with wide-open windows, and porches. Marijuana plants poured over ledges, giving slight shade to businesses below. Above, women and boys pranced back and forth, each more skimpily dressed than the next. The women rolled their shoulders and blew kisses at the crowd, baring a breast at anyone who looked back, and many did, as the nearly naked boys did cartwheels or wrestled with one another to display their prowess and form.

"Prostitutes," Hardy pointed out. "Each second floor is occupied by a family of prostitutes, mostly mothers, daughters, and sons. But those with a husband or wife usually run the stalls below, cooking, knocking a head or two if the customers get too rowdy. When their children lose their looks, they can help out in the kitchen or go fishing."

Scallop explained that "go fishing" actually meant to disappear, to leave the island and find your own way in the world—that young men and women often left Marathon to join the Kudzu Army, returning on holiday to show off their strong backs and spend their money, or "Jump," as it was called in the keys. But just as many left their families while still quite young and lived as dive boys, sleeping on the beach, seeking quick highs, tattooing one another's backs, diving for lost anchors or untangling crab traps for easy Jump, rolling with the waves, and rarely living past the age of twenty.

One similarity to Last Bridge: at nearly every step, they were interrupted by dirty children who ran obliviously through the streets, squealing and laughing, chasing each other, daring one another to steal a bottle of rum from the street vendors. As the boys neared the center of town, they noted fewer children. Old men and women lounged in the long shadows of giant banyan trees. Ropey roots unwound from thick canopies to screw into the ground and harden, making each tree a collection of hovels and shadows. The old men and women withered beneath their rags, their flesh hung from their bones, scorched by the sun and polished by sweat into the same wooden color of the tree that claimed them. Most were passed-out drunk but shot gnarled hands out as the boys neared, mouthing toothless cries of rage and want, despair or delusion. Fewer peddlers sold seared fish on skewers, and most businesses here had thick saloon doors. Leaf recognized the symbols of gambling halls, but not all of the stalls were makeshift casinos. Cursing carpenters and dour blacksmiths served contentious customers. The buildings were crowned with rickety windmills, a churning forest that creaked and moaned.

Hardy pointed to the windmills.

"When it gets dark, there's electricity."

For the first time in Leaf's life, he looked forward to challenging the night.

THEY PASSED THROUGH THE CENTER of town. Yet another massive banyan tree spread a swath of interlaced branches, beneath which numerous members of the Coast Guard slumbered in hammocks, their machetes hung from tree limbs. Children slept on the ground in the coolness of the sailors' shadows. At the hottest part of the day, Marathon retired for siesta, and Hardy promised to show them the beach on the other side of the island. Scallop and Hardy freely perspired as they all walked a strange lane, black, cracked asphalt, fissures filled with sand and trampled weed, that emerged as the island narrowed; the huts crowding the beach petered out. Eventually, the road ran into the ocean. A rust-eaten stop sign listed in the water.

Hardy wriggled out of his shorts as if they were an annoying, confining thing and rushed the waves naked, arms out. Scallop stripped and followed. Leaf lay down, ran his fingers through the sand, and lifted his face to focus on the sun. His cheeks flared.

His eyelids fluttered. With a deep breath, he felt light penetrate his expanding chest; his knees absorbed sunlight and stored the power like twin batteries. Stroking the white petals at his neck, he watched the boys roll in the surf.

When they tired and stumbled ashore, water streaked off their bodies. Scallop collapsed and rolled onto his side, and his breathing quickly slowed. Hardy remained standing, his bulging stomach muscles tumbled into a wet thicket of dark hair spackled with seaweed. As he examined Hardy, Leaf's stamen twitched with curiosity against its protective leaf. The other boy's penis hung low, weighty, ending with a knot of loose foreskin.

He settled on the sand beside Leaf, who looked at both boys in comparison. Scallop's knees were braided with scars from brushing coral and the other hazards of fishing, while Hardy had various well-healed cuts all over his body, though some were jagged and seemed violent, unnatural. Leaf fingered the shark's tooth necklace that hung low on his chest. He had no scars and wondered what cuts the future had in store for him. He put his head down, and the three rested in the sun. Every subtle movement further coated them in periwinkles of sand and tiny shards of shell.

SCALLOP ROSE ON AN ELBOW and surveyed the breaking surf. Far away, an old man under an umbrella hat wheeled a cart through the sand.

To Hardy, "You got any jump?"

"Sure." Hardy turned on his side and rummaged through the pockets of his crumpled shorts. Leaf noticed that the imprint of his bare buttocks in the sand formed two serene pools of shadow.

Hardy handed Scallop some coins, and Scallop leaped up, deftly pulled his loincloth on, and ran down the beach. As Scallop chased after the old man, Hardy reclined, spreading his legs and pushing his heels into the sand. His thighs were dark green, with fewer scales than his chest and back. With his finger, Leaf traced the outline of a large plate on Hardy's shoulder. The plate was hard but definitely flesh—a natural armor. Hardy sighed. He rolled his heels in the sand, flexing his thighs to draw attention to the growing thickness between his legs. Leaf drew a line down Hardy's chest and toward his stomach with his finger. Scallop gave a whoop of success and approached with two bottles foaming with ginger beer. Hardy shot Leaf a quick smile and rolled onto his stomach. Sand evenly sugared his butt cheeks. Scallop dropped to his knees, gave Hardy a beer, and offered Leaf a sip from his bottle. The brown, sweaty glass was shockingly cool in Leaf's hand. He looked quizzically at Scallop.

"Ice."

"Impossible."

"No, there's an ice factory behind the Coast Guard station. It's one of the things that makes Marathon special. Also, it's the only place they make Jump." He held up a coin between two fingers.

A conch emblazoned by the sun. He flipped it into the air, and Leaf caught it. It wasn't as heavy as he thought it would be. He pinched it between his fingers and felt it was formed from several different metals.

Scallop intuited: "Yeah, any metal you find, you can trade for fresh water, bread, after the Coast Guard weighs it. And to keep things clean, they don't take any themselves. They get paid only when their term of service ends, though they're allowed to eat for free in any of the shops, and the fishermen give them their extra catch."

"Do people steal jump?"

"Sure, every day, and if you get caught, they cut your hand off. Do it again, the Coast Guard hangs you."

Leaf looked shocked. Hardy sat up and crossed his legs. After a big swallow of beer, he took over the conversation.

"I've only seen one hanging in all my years here, once when I was a little boy, and it was horrible." His face was blank, serious as if he was summoning more than a memory.

"It wasn't over money, no. It was religion. My Mom took me. The whole island turned out. And it was just some poor sailor mad from the sun ranting about…Christ." He whispered the name as if a foul belch crossed his lips.

"They hung him from the big banyan tree, pulled back the tire swing my friends, and I played on so there'd be room. Of course, everyone knew he was crazy, that they were doing it to set an example. Religion started the Red War, people say."

Hardy took a long drink. Scallop shaded his eyes with his hands, quietly searching the vast sea. Hardy stood and walked toward the water to wash off the sand. Scallop dropped to a squat.

"Hardy's dad left the island because he was caught stealing someone's jump. It's okay if you come back after a few years, but he never did. That's why he joined the Kudzu Army, not for the jump but for the jump he stole."

"My nanny told me the Red War was started by governments, not religion."

"Yeah, I heard that, too. And look: now we don't have either."

Scallop stood again and watched Hardy. The arrow of the other boy's body rode a wave cresting toward shore. Scallop looked past him, out toward the dark ocean, flecked with distant white waves. He was searching for his father. Remote waves crushed against each other, against nothing, their angry spray rising and sinking into the wind.

Leaf wondered what would have happened if he had continued to touch Hardy and if the touch of another would make the same subtle indentations as the sun, nourishing and warm, and yet leave scars as well.

※

As the boys walked back toward town, they talked about Canal City. The petals around Leaf's neck drooped as Scallop and Hardy detailed how slavers sold captured souls to the King

Pelicans—the sinister birds had conspired to return water and electricity to the wreckage of Miami. They drove an army of conscripts to fight against the constant fury of kudzu writhing across the south, pouring down from the nuclear craters of North Carolina. Growing several yards a day, known to strangle cattle where they stood, the mutant vines threatened the largest source of fresh water in Florida, Lake Okeechobee. The slaves provided a human aqueduct. All passed through Canal City before heading to the swamp oblivion.

Hardy listed what he could contribute to the mission, recommending places where they could buy cheap bread and tackle.

Scallop was encouraged by Hardy's enthusiasm. His mood had lightened considerably when they reached Marathon; Leaf had even thought he might abandon this quest, Hardy's energy redoubled Scallop's determination to find his father: they would leave in the morning. Leaf shivered at the thought of monster birds above and miles of insatiable vine ever surging toward them. He felt trapped between two impossible evils engaged in a battle that, no matter which side prevailed, darkness won.

The siesta had ended when they arrived at the center of town.

Peddlers pushed odd carts cobbled together from wheelbarrows and children's bicycles, selling sweetened jellyfish, iced coconut milk, and fish skewers. Cranky windmills spun. A blind, drooling beggar reached toward Leaf, but Hardy placed a protective arm around his shoulder. As the crowd thickened, the three of them linked arms. Leaf asked Hardy where he lived, and Hardy shot him an incredulous look.

"Here. All of Marathon is home, I guess." Hardy shook his head in exasperation.

"Hardy sleeps on the beach, all the dive boys do. And the fishermen sleep in their boats, the Coast Guard sleep in their hammocks. Only the hookers sleep indoors at night, and I bet they're not getting much sleep." Scallop giggled, and Hardy poked Leaf in the ribs to show he didn't think he was too much the alien.

But Leaf's mood turned serious.

"Well, I sleep outside, too, Scallop. And the minute it gets dark, I won't have a choice of when or where, so we need to find a place soon."

He looked back toward the beggar on the ground, clawing at the air. "And one of you has to watch over me."

Scallop patted his arm. "Wait a minute, Leaf. You haven't seen anything until you've seen Marathon at night, and I guarantee you'll be able to see it."

Hardy took them to a place where he knew the cook, promising them a meal of marlin steaks and Key Lime pie. As dusk stained the sky purple, the streets filled with more people. Fishermen and dive boys returned from the sea. With his bent and worn fork, Scallop pointed toward the windmills, and Leaf turned. They twinkled lightly against the purple clouds.

"Eee-lect-ricity, baby," Hardy said with a wink and a full mouth. Leaf felt sluggish as the sun was going down, but at the same time, curious about the artificial lights that began to dot the ramshackle skyline of Marathon.

"I don't know if electricity will be enough to keep him awake," Scallop said, chewing another mouthful, ever watchful for the waitress to bring him more iced tea; since they had been seated,

Scallop had fretted they would run out of pie before he had a chance to order. Hardy let out another belch.

"Don't worry, they never run out of pie. They smother it with coconut milk. It's amazing." He, too, looked around. Half-standing, he motioned for two slices of pie.

He turned to Leaf, "It's the full moon tonight. Does that affect you?"

"I don't know. I've never purposefully tried to stay awake."

"Really? 'Cause, it affects us!"

He snorted, and Scallop nodded knowingly and eagerly. More people traipsed down the street. Men bent beneath dripping nets thick with wide-eyed fish. What a world these panting fish saw, Leaf thought: the insanely turning coral of the windmills, an ocean of blue sky, desperately out-of-reach, a sinister illusion of home; if they could break free and launch themselves into the air, they would still suffocate, twisting and twisting and turning in painful incomprehension until they smacked against the dirty ground.

The boys left the steamy cooking shack and tumbled back onto the street. Music filled the air. At first, Leaf thought it was the sing-song conversation particular to Marathon. The people of the island possessed a rainbow of pet birds, and he thought the sounds were coming from the cages that hung from the verandas of prostitutes. He stopped short, jerking his companions to a halt as well.

Leaf found this sound nearly as intoxicating as the sun. He stood still and listened, fording the din to pinpoint the source.

He wanted it to come to him as sunlight did, directly, consistently, but it flitted with the incense and cooking-fire-infused breeze. His face contorted in ecstasy and confusion as the boys tightened their grip on him and hurried through the throng.

Electric lights flickered on. Strings of light lit the banisters above the stalls and cafes. The sky darkened further, and the windmills became dim crazy suns. Though Leaf was sleepy, the pull of the music and the sound of electricity blooming across the island fed Leaf sporadic morsels of energy and kept him awake. For the first time, he was going to see the night. Another world he had never before considered visiting. Night in a filthy island city rife with undulating waves of people filtering this new, fluid, intoxicating source of light. Leaf wondered if this was the world Skate knew, an orchestra of shells tumbling like bells in the wash of the waves above the flourishing neon flowers that shape sharp reefs. He slipped his soft hand into Hardy's hard, calloused palm.

As they left the city behind, the crowd did not ease, but the lights dimmed, and so did Leaf. They tumbled through the dunes, and Hardy greeted friends who passed frothy brown bottles of rum to him and Scallop. Near the shore, a large open fire roared. Leaf imbibed this light as the boys sloshed rum. While electricity gave Leaf a plastic consistency, muted but useful, the fire felt untamed, as if burning lions from the jungles of the sun had angrily sprouted on earth. Leaf felt the uncontrolled pulse of a white heart, ravenous, straining against a cage of crackling boards. Assaulted by such raw power, he was drawn closer.

And the music was louder, fluid—it moved with the fire.

Naked dive boys beat drums, backs sweaty from the proximity to flame. Girls with bronze breasts bounced up and down, braided hair lashing their faces. They pulled their short skirts farther down their tattooed waists. An old woman with silver hair as long and furious as tangled fishnet went mad on a flute.

Fat-bellied children with lost, happy eyes clapped to the beat.

Leaf slipped away from his friends and rushed to the fire. He sensed the danger of coming too close and backed away into one of the dancers. Instead of being angry, she took his hands, and they spun together. She released him with a dreamy smile as a boy in a grass skirt took him up and put his hands on Leaf's waist while shaking his head back and forth. His arms were as skinny as Leaf's. The boy's movements were in perfect accord with the drums. His boney hips separated the folds of grass as he shimmied and shook, and his feet kicked up the feather-soft sand.

A flash of green. Hardy twirled past naked. As he turned, firelight played off his flesh, knife-like shadows cut from his nipples to his shoulders. His teeth glowed and flickered between parted lips, and his head wavered back and forth, slowly, like an alligator calmly paddling toward its prey. Scallop moved between them. He was dancing with a tall, beautiful girl, naked save a pink T-shirt smeared with grime, cut high above her shaved and tattooed pubis. His long fingers danced across her stomach while she gripped the back of his head by his wiry hair.

The sound intensified as more drummers joined the circle.

Bottles of beer and rum were passed back and forth. Acrid smoke rose as children lit joints against the massive, booming fire. Leaf's partner twirled away as Leaf waved his arms in the air.

He then lowered his hands, palms out, and felt the nearness of the fire while he danced. He wanted to scoop out balls of light and juggle them like dainty stars and imagined that they would singe his hands only slightly. Hypnotized and ready for pain, he moved closer to the fire, but Hardy came up from behind and spun him, so they were face to sweaty face. Leaf's eyes were crazed molten pools of amber that cooled beneath Hardy's gaze of wry amusement.

Hardy moved one shoulder to the beat of the drums, then the other, bending backward slowly, thrusting his hips rhythmically toward Leaf, pinning him against the wall of heat that emanated from the fire. Leaf would have panicked if the music had not pulled him toward the other boy. He placed his palms on Hardy's hard hips and moved closer, synchronizing their sway and beat.

Hardy bent toward Leaf and gripped his waist, fingers playing lightly across his lower back, the length of his penis brushing against Leaf's bare thigh. Putting his finger to his lips, he tasted Leaf's sweat. A look of astonishment brightened his face.

"You taste sweet," he whispered.

"Nectar," Leaf replied and spun in his arms.

The old woman with the flute came up beside them and wove a honeycomb of sound. Her hair shimmered like a thousand minnows caught in gray shallows. The dancers moved with the song and for each other. Hardy's eyes were locked on Leaf's, who measured Hardy's thick, chapped lips with dry fingers, then the muscular cords that anchored his neck, but the drums pulled his head back, and he looked through the smoke to see stars. Their light was too old to nourish him, so he looked back at the spark in Hardy's eyes. The moon shone through, its dry sea beds and marble cities consumed by sandstorms casting a pale pall.

They reluctantly separated, and Leaf spun slowly, the animal light of the fire clawing at different parts of his body, feeding his entire being. The drumming slowed. Someone passed Leaf a warm bottle of beer, and he finished the last saliva-heavy mouthful.

Someone else tried to hand him a joint, but the closeness of burning foliage repulsed him, and he moved to the edge of the circle.

As he watched, couples formed. Groups groped, pouring beer over each other, then kissing and licking body parts. Dark figures joined in the churning shallows of the surf. Scallop was with the same girl from earlier. They had wandered half into the black water. She was naked as he kissed her breasts and slowly pulled on himself. Moonlight caressed the waves.

Gunshots from town stilled the drums. Everyone paused. The fire cracked and flickered as the burning driftwood shifted and sparks swirled upwards in the smoke. The woman with the flute played a short lament, then the drums renewed with fervent, pounding joy. Hardy danced with a girl. They kissed a deliberate, eternal kiss, rum passing back and forth between their mouths.

Then the drums beat a different path, and she pulled away and joined a chain of children circling the fire. Hardy looked for Leaf and smiled when he spotted him on the edge of the dancers.

As he approached, Leaf's spine arched, alert to a new and different sound. He followed it and saw a man inside the ring of dancing children strumming a guitar. The drums began to wrap around his resonance. Applause erupted. Hardy reached for Leaf, and they kissed fiercely. Leaf's legs ran in place to the beat as their lips crashed into each other. Hardy's tongue slid against Leaf's as they drank each other's breath: Hardy's was fire-hot, acidic, and alcoholic, Leaf's rainwater and honey. Hardy's eyelashes fluttered against Leaf's cheeks like black Monarch butterflies.

This was Leaf's first kiss. The singular white leaf that clasped his groin rolled away as his stamen unfurled. Hardy felt this against his own growth and looked down and then back up and into Leaf's wide and curious eyes.

"You be the flower, I'll be the bee," he whispered breathlessly as he lowered himself.

Gently, he took the stalk into his mouth. His tongue explored the thrice-ridged reed. He followed it to its sharp conclusion and there rhythmically nursed and teethed. Leaf's fingers gripped the stiff, sea salt-encrusted hair of the boy below and blindly combed his scalp. Hardy grasped Leaf's buttocks to calm his still-dancing legs. Leaf no longer thought of the drums as he followed the music of Hardy's mouth. He watched as Hardy's strong back muscles flexed and his feet dug deeper into the sand.

All around, couples kissed and pulled at one another. Entanglements of flesh ground into the sand. The fire painted them in undulating shadows. In the surf, Scallop steadied himself and faced Leaf as his girl, too, went down. They gazed at each other knowingly, initiates of the night. And Leaf felt a tightness and an impending rush of internal heat. He rose on his toes and clenched his fists with Hardy's hair between his fingers. His eyes fluttered as Hardy held him closer, ready for something the other boy could yet not comprehend. Leaf looked into the fire and found its white core as this new heat rose within him, flared out, and Hardy swallowed and moaned while both their bodies quaked with delight. His lips tightened, begging Leaf for more, so he gave it to him. Another bolt of flame gathered beneath his stomach and poured out. Hardy gasped. Leaf let go of his hair and looked up. The stars above seemed closer, expectant.

Hardy's own warmth spilled onto Leaf's sandy toes. The gently crashing waves were louder than the now-lone drummer who sat somewhere unseen, providing the dive boys and their momentary lovers with a final, tender beat.

The old woman with the flute emerged naked from the surf. Her flesh caved in on itself like the upturned hull of a shipwrecked boat. She looked startled and surprised to have made land as if she had forgotten her role in the bacchanal or those other people were even involved. Stumbling forward, she stopped and looked at each and every couple, finding their eyes, silently imploring them to listen. She came close to the fire for warmth and inspiration.

Her hair was heavy, drenched, and laden with tendrils of black seaweed. She commenced playing her song.

It was a command, an ancient call to battle, a song last heard in a grove of gray pine needles trampled by boys with fresh hooves chasing green girls with gentle garlands as well as each other. Hardy fell back and shielded his eyes as if blinded by an approaching comet. Couples tore apart or rejoined with animal fury. A woman screamed an empty, maternal howl. Drunken men patted the sand for their discarded drum sticks and obediently took up the beat. And Leaf stood and blossomed.

The song stoked the heat in his heart, and his stamen again stood firm, not robbed of its pollen but freshly tapped. It pulsed and extended farther. White seed leaked out. Hardy rolled in the sand, mouth opening and closing in silence. A young girl, transfixed by the reflection of the fire in Leaf's eyes, reverently lowered herself before him and gingerly tasted his bud. She gasped, pulled back, wild-eyed, and then fervently renewed her ministrations. The boy with whom Leaf had danced earlier joined her, kissing Leaf's thighs, politely nuzzling her out of his way with little nips and moans. Hardy rose on his knees and joined Leaf, steadying

him with a strong arm bracing his buttocks as others gathered to taste and
worship. Leaf could smell his own honeyed sweetness on the breath of
those whispering and kissing each other at his knees.

Children rushed wood to the fire to keep them all in the light.

The drums stayed steady. More and more dive boys knelt at Leaf's
feet. Those at the back kissed the newly anointed and sighed at the mere
taste. Leaf's eyes were often closed at the wonderful feeling of feeding so
many, but once, when they fluttered open, he sought out Scallop.

He was still positioned in the dark surf with his girl. They embraced,
staring at Leaf with suspicion or wonderment; he couldn't tell in the
flickering light and smoke. Leaf's lips parted—he thought to call to his
friend, but he didn't know if he wanted to invite him to partake or change
places. The fire crackled and flared, and Leaf turned back toward its raw
yet supple light, but not before noticing Scallop's grip on the girl's wrists.
He wasn't holding her with affection. He was holding her back.

PART

TWO

I THOUGHT I
WAS NOT ALONE
WALKING HERE
BY THE SHORE

WALT WHITMAN

TIDE AND TRAVEL

IN THE MORNING, LEAF WALKED the beach as boats headed out to sea. Dive boys scrambled past him to join the fishermen. Fresh smoke wove down the beach into the azure sky as cooking fires were stoked. Babies cried. Leaf turned as Scallop jogged up behind him.

"Hey, we should try to get an early start."

Scallop paused to catch his breath. Bent over, hands on his knees, he looked up and searched Leaf's face. Without any change in his outward appearance, his friend had grown, and Scallop didn't know how to address it. He had been to many full moon parties on Marathon, but none had ever ended quite like the previous night. Leaf smiled back. He had woken far from the smoldering fire and remembered drifting on a sea of arms, gingerly hoisted by yearning palms. He had kissed so many and was kissed in turn, everywhere. Sunlight erased bite marks from his thighs and chest, and hickeys dissipated from his slender neck. Scallop rose and dusted sand off his elbows and looked out to sea.

"Are you tired?"

"I am never tired. You know that."

"Yeah, but I figured… I figure I should get something to eat. Let's walk into town."

Leaf nodded and followed. More boats put to sea, and Scallop's head turned with each one as his pace quickened.

As they entered the already crowded street, Hardy called to them from among the throng, vigorously waving one arm. Scallop didn't notice as he was distracted by a group of fisherman hoisting the carcass of a hammerhead shark up on a pulley by the docks. A haze of flies obscured the bleeding crescent of its mouth. Leaf put his hand on Scallop's shoulder to get his attention and felt him involuntarily flinch. To compensate, Scallop placed his hand on the small of Leaf's back as they stood on their toes to see above the bobbing multitude.

"Have I got something for you!" Hardy announced, pushing past people to appear before them like a new, green sun. He shone. A triumphant smile lit his face, his hair wild, blond palm fronds hurricane-tossed. One hand held a rusty pail of salt water while the other cradled Skate, adhering to his chest, two eager eyes penetrating, imploring Leaf with a thousand questions and exclamations.

"Skate!"

Leaf rushed to them both and dropped to his knees. Skate fluttered with delight. Leaf gently brushed him and sensed his journey, read his ripples, and drew from his eyes the tale Hardy would surely tell, and as he did so, he placed one hand on Hardy's taut stomach and absently picked at the rind of last night's nectar which caked his bellybutton.

"But how?" Leaf inquired.

Hardy swung the bucket into Scallop's arms and hoisted Skate like a trophy.

"I was coming back from the market." He shot Scallop a quick look. "I'd gotten us a deal on bread and went to collect some overdue jump from a fisherman."

Scallop gave his typical nod of approval. Leaf dipped his cupped hands into the bucket and lovingly poured water over Skate, who quivered in appreciation, his gaze never leaving Leaf's.

"So I was over by the big dock when I heard some fishermen shouting about this strange ray. I walked over and asked what was going on. Now, they know me, I've dove for most of them, and this guy, still in his boat, just looked spooked and crazy and excited all at once, and he's holding up Skate here, still in a net, for everyone to see. Well, of course, I saw his human eyes. We all did! Everyone was talking about it; some fisherman are yelling, 'Throw it back, throw it back,' and 'They don't call 'em devil fish for nothin', cut it up!'"

Skate's eyes went up and down in rapid agreement. Hardy eased him into the bucket of water.

"But the fisherman just told everyone to be quiet and said, 'Here, listen! It talks.' And sure enough, he held Skate higher, and damned if he didn't croak, 'Leaf, Leaf.' Well, the crowd went wild. Someone called for the Coast Guard, and I jumped into the boat. See, this was the guy who owed me Jump. I had retrieved his anchor for him in some serious water, and he'd never paid me. But I know him; he's a little slow and doesn't like confrontation.

So I told him, 'You owe me Jump, but I'll take fish, this fish!'—slit the net and jumped overboard before anyone had a chance to say anything."

Skate blinked in admiration.

"And when I dove, I made like I was heading toward shore, but with Skate here suctioned to my chest for dear life, I doubled back under the boat and surfaced under the dock, treading water until things calmed down. Fishermen will gossip and fight and argue, but when the tide's going out, so do they, so I didn't have to wait long."

"Skate, I didn't know you could talk!" Surprised, Leaf looked at Skate, who just rolled his eyes and shook his body back and forth in the negative. Scallop was thrilled to see Skate even as he lightly bounced on the backs of his heels. Hardy sensed his unease.

"Let me get something from the blacksmith that will make today a whole lot easier. Scallop, if you can go to the baker's, the last on the strip, you know the one with the crooked sign?

Good. She said she'd sell whatever bread she had left over after high tide to us at half-price." Scallop had already pivoted in that direction.

"Go, we'll meet back here at half-tide."

Scallop started off at a half-jog, stopped, turned and scooped his hand in the bucket of water, and massaged a handful onto Skate's rough hide. Then he was off. Skate closed his eyes and rested as Hardy and Leaf walked toward the center of town. Hardy's arm on Leaf's shoulder felt as right and warm as the sun on his back.

Hardy borrowed an ancient red wagon from a blacksmith he knew. It had been painted and re-painted numerous times to stave off the rust that deformed its cranky axle and twisted handle. They filled it with seawater, plopped Skate in, and waded through the crowd: Marathon was an original sea of people who dyed themselves colors, kept birds in their hair, and decorated their backs with the tattoos of fish never caught, a mosaic of imagined shells and mates and maidens long gone. Occasionally someone who had been blessed or cursed by the touch of a gene box wand would surface: exceptionally long arms swung spidery hands with a multitude of fingers. A girl with gills pushed past; the fin atop her head cut through the crowd like a baby shark cruising toward its mother. It was with unique pride everyone ignored two green boys pulling a wagon wherein sloshed a ray with searching human eyes. Dive boys from last night, however, seemed to be making an effort to pass close by. Fingers brushed Leaf's hips and lingered. Hardy sensed this and growled and bared his teeth at a few boys as they approached. At the bait shop, he haggled for tackle, demanded an extra ration of water from the depot, the town's lone brackish well, paid for some oranges with his last Jump, and steered Leaf and Skate back toward the meeting place well before the appointed time.

"Will we take your boat or Scallop's?" Leaf asked.

"What makes you think I have a boat? You assume everyone already has everything, Leaf. It's just not so." He traced the shiny new hooks with his finger and did not look at Leaf when he spoke. His words, designed to hurt, missed their mark.

"No, Hardy, that's not true. Please remember that you may be the fourth person I've spoken to in my life. So I think I'm doing pretty good for all that's happened here."

Then softly, he added, "But what about your assumptions, about me?" Leaf tilted his head, a curious, emerald moon orbiting the answer.

Hardy looked up at the sky. "Well, I don't have any. Well, I have one." And he looked at Leaf, narrowing his eyes, and a smile parted his lips. Their eyes locked. His pupils were fluid, mother-of-pearl, Leaf's swirling reflection in them peripheral, like a storm far out at sea. Scallop approached with a sack over his shoulder, a fishing spear in his hand.

"We should go."

"Sure, but let's wait for the tide to turn." Hardy reached for the spear and rolled it in his hands.

"No, we should go now. People are talking about last night." Scallop was resolute.

Hardy shrugged and pretended to aim the spear. Its point wavered a bit too close to Skate, who gave him a flustered splash; the silence between the boys grew problematic.

Eventually, Hardy retorted, "So what? Full moon is always like that."

He held up the spear and looked down its length. "Well, last night was especially wild, but dive boys are dive boys, and I saw you getting your salt on, too, you know." Satisfied, he handed the spear back to Scallop.

Scallop gritted his teeth. "But everyone is talking about Leaf. Everyone who went up to him last night is saying that they feel different, uh—better."

People on the edge of the square did seem to notice them. Their whispered names rose above the gossip.

"Especially that guy," Scallop jerked his head toward the handless beggar. Leaf looked at him, dirty, crawling on the ground trailing rags, his sunburned face askew on a leathery neck. Leaf did not remember him from the previous night; so many people had swarmed about. He wasn't surprised or offended, so he shrugged to demonstrate his indifference to Scallop and Hardy.

"It's not that—it's what he's saying."

A woman brought the beggar some overcooked fish and listened patiently while he told his tale. They could not hear what he said but saw that he was tearful and exuberant. He waved his arms crazily to display new, springtime buds. Little stubs emerged from his ruined wrists: pink fingers grew, pushing through like bamboo shoots. Hardy's jaw dropped. Scallop gave them both a shove.

"Guys, let's get to the boat."

SEVERAL DIVE BOYS HAD GATHERED expectantly on the beach. The boy Leaf had danced with shyly approached. Hardy was about to step between them when the boy held out cupped hands.

A radiant hibiscus rested in his palms, the white petals kissed by rot with a central churn of orange. A lone bee drifted above his head. The girl Leaf had danced with came forward and placed the hibiscus behind his ear. They each kissed him on the cheek.

Scallop ignored all of this, pulled the wagon to the water's edge, and dumped its stagnating contents, freeing Skate. Dirty, naked children squatted and stared at Leaf. Scallop caught their attention with some shiny jump, flipped a coin toward the lot of them, and told the one who caught it to take the cart back to the blacksmith. Hardy had one foot in the surf, ready for the next adventure. Skate circled him excitedly. Hardy held his hand out to Leaf, who wavered. Scallop plunged into the waves, surfaced, and called out to Leaf.

"Just stay here; we'll be back with the skiff. We'll get it as close as possible. C'mon, Hardy."

A splash from Skate broke Hardy's gaze. Hoisting the supplies above the water with one hand, he slowly followed after Scallop. Leaf watched his strong back cut through the surf. Foam flowed between the wide cracks of the scales that bunched at the back of his neck. More people gathered around: dive boys from last night squatted close to shore and openly stared at him.

A girl with blue mandalas tattooed on her cheeks absent-mindedly braided her stringy black hair while looking at Leaf with wonder. Two members of the Coast Guard marched down the beach, bare-chested in dark blue sarongs, machetes slapping their thighs in unison.

Leaf inched toward the water but was hesitant about swimming alone. The boys had reached the boat, raised the sail, and sped toward the beach. Several disfigured beggars broke through the growing crowd, calling out raspy inanities. Both feet in the water, Leaf nearly swooned as the refracted sunlight pulled at him like cheap wine. The Coast Guard pushed the beggars to the sand and lunged at Leaf as he fell into the surf and swam lazily toward the skiff. Scallop marshaled the sail and tacked just so. The boat turned as it approached, lifting Leaf in its wake and into Hardy's waiting hands. With a gentle tap on the butt from Skate, Leaf was hoisted aboard, and they were off, sailing to Canal City. A band of young pirates ready to raid the future, unsure if it would plunder them as well, their sail bountiful with hopeful wind. Marathon quickly receded behind them. They faced the open water with a steady hand at the tiller, eager, anxious, and resolute, Skate happily surfing the bow as the waters deepened and the sea darkened.

GHOST
MERIDIAN

As the boys sailed across the water, Leaf listened intently to the music of the sail's fabric roiled like a soft drum, and the boat rhythmically sliced the waves. A giddy pod of chattering dolphins broke the surface close enough that the boys could see their elliptic reflections in inquisitive black eyes. Skate rolled in the wake, then rested by suctioning himself to the hull. Hardy's hair burned in the wind. Scallop scanned the horizon for danger, slavers, sandbars, and answers. Concern lined his face. The dolphins tired as the day progressed and left them. Aft, Hardy extended his rear as much as possible to shit overboard. Scallop tugged at the tiller, and the boat wobbled. Hardy laughed and pretended as if he were about to fall overboard. Scallop smiled, but the lines on his forehead remained. The sun painted Leaf with life, light, and energy.

Depending on the wind, the journey from Marathon to Canal City typically took two days. Rising tides had long ago consumed the majority of the middle keys. They would see little land and what was available above Marathon was best avoided.

Their skiff skirted Deer Key, a thin ribbon of sand and mangrove.

Deer Key was the Leper Colony. The only people to head south from the mainland were lepers. Leprosy was transmitted from soil, not sand, so no outbreak had ever struck the keys. However, the island was typically avoided out of fear and prejudice, a benefit to the miniature key deer that resided there, making it the last outpost for their fragile species. Scallop tacked to circumvent a boat-shredding reef and brought the boys unusually close to the island. As they sailed past, a boy in rags raised a gray, fingerless hand in mute greeting. A startled miniature doe leaped from before the leper's feet, noted the skiff's progress, and slipped into a copse of stunted pine. Their eyes shone the same: Deer Key was their entire world, the boys in the boat intangible, just one of many passing clouds.

After a few measly sand bars, no more islands, no seagulls. They faced the open sea. The afternoon was quiet. Scallop, without the distraction of Marathon, meditated on what lay ahead. Hardy fished, content whether he caught anything or not. Leaf basked in the sun.

HARDY PULLED IN HIS FISHING line and swung to face Leaf. A wisp of hair played against his forehead. Jokingly, he swiped at the hibiscus still miraculously tucked behind Leaf's ear. Laughing, Leaf ducked, but Hardy caught it but could not pull it free.

Mutually curious, Leaf bent down and let him bend back the fold of his ear. The flower had taken root. Hardy squinted, made a quick decision, and pulled. With effort, he uprooted the flower.

Leaf immediately patted down the torn flesh behind his ear while Hardy examined the clumps of green matter which clung to the long roots.

"I want to do something." He leaned closer. Leaf looked over at Scallop, determined behind the tiller.

Sly Hardy tilted his head. "No, not that, not yet, at least. But tell me if this hurts." And he took a fish hook and slowly pierced Leaf's thumb. They both watched as it knocked politely at his fingernail before emerging out the other side.

"Holy shit, you didn't feel that? You don't feel pain?" A disturbing flash of excitement lit up his eyes.

"No. Or maybe not in the way you do, though. I felt the hook, but it wasn't paining for me; it felt like an absence of light."

But Leaf had felt so many other things since leaving his island.

He tried to communicate this to Hardy with his eyes. Hardy smiled, but shame crossed his cheeks: he had accidentally crushed the flower in his hands. He quickly seasoned the ocean with ruined petals and leaves.

"Let me take the hook out, Leaf. I'm sorry. Maybe this trip—I've never been this far out, I've never been without Marathon in my sight before."

He reached toward Leaf, who swiftly removed the hook and tossed it overboard. A green bubble ballooned from the opening on his thumb. Scallop looked as if he were about to say something but remained silent, sullen. Hardy took Leaf's thumb into his mouth. Leaf closed his eyes. He felt like the sun. Again, he radiated. For all the years that he absorbed light, he now spent some. Hardy sighed and relaxed against the side of the boat. His lips were wet with saliva. The boat hit a rough wave, and everyone adjusted their position. Hardy shifted. He found a pillow in Leaf's lap, relaxed, and soaked up the sun. And, of course, so too did Leaf.

THE WIND CALMED AS DUSK approached; Scallop searched for an uninhabited island to call their own for the night. He noted a speck on the horizon and pointed the skiff in that direction.

Hardy stared hard at the distant island. Agitated, he crawled all over the boat.

"Do you know where we are?" he said to Scallop.

"Of course I do. And we're going to have to spend the night there."

Hardy stood and balled his fists. "If that's what I think it is, I don't want to."

"No one ever does, which is why it's a good place to camp."

Hardy pouted, turned to Leaf, and mouthed 'Vampire Key.'

Every child who grew up in the Keys knew the story of the Lamprey children. Nanny told Leaf the tale at sunset. Scallop's father threatened him with their vengeance if he didn't eat his evening meal. The dive boys of Marathon re-enacted their tale around dying fires on chilly moonless nights. So much of the world was lost after the Red War, yet this Florida yarn remained and gained strength, stitching the fragile islands together with a cobweb of fear. So many of the old links had eroded.

Scallop tacked toward land. Scraggly pines picked at the coral sky like nervous fingers as the island grew. Eerily, no birds hovered near shore. Hardy busied himself with the tackle and needlessly rearranged supplies. They circled Vampire Key. A small island, its shore was unwelcoming, with little beach. Insular snarls of dark mangrove bored into the sand. Thick, knife-like mollusks gathered at the roots, extended into the water, and threatened to damage the bottom of the skiff.

Scallop was surprised to learn that Leaf knew the tale as they compared versions and noted differences. Hardy chimed in with accounts most popular on Marathon. They busily dissected the myth; doing so in no way diminished the power it had over them as children, for they had never considered that they would hazard spending the night on Vampire Key.

The story of the Lamprey children and their cursed lives on the now Atlantean Key West was a tale of past riches and dark familial woe. After the death of their parents (and the boys had wildly divergent versions of their passing: lightning / drowning / shark) they were sent to live with a wealthy uncle who possessed a terrible secret. One night while hiding behind a curtain (giant fern / luminous statue), the children discovered that their aloof uncle cultivated the rarest of orchids, a diaphanous jewel of ruby petals that only flourished when fed human blood under the light of the full moon—its provider would be blessed with immortality. As the denizens of Key West succumbed to the uncle's bloodlust, the horrified Lamprey children acted. They stole the orchid to end its evil hold over the island and fled by boat (train / automobile, though oddly, only Leaf knew what a train was, leading to a momentary, incredulous digression). Their uncle pursued them to a remote, as yet unnamed, key. To the children's horror and uncle's delight, they accidentally led him to the island where he had discovered the night blossom. In a monstrous rage, he killed them both and drained their blood, throwing their rendered bodies into the sea. His fury never subsided. No longer human, he remained on the island to guard his precious orchids, murdering any who came ashore, watering the thirsty flower with the blood of innocent sailors (fisherman, dive boys hoping to make it big in Canal City). The ghosts of the Lamprey children, ever trying to warn lost fishermen seeking shelter for the night, rapped a warning on the bottom of their boats.

Waves lapped the hull as the boys finished the collective telling of the tale. Just as Hardy whispered the last words, a soft, deliberate knocking haunted the underside of the skiff. The boys jumped. Hesitantly, Hardy put his ear to the bottom of the boat, then shot back as a loud knock shook the planks. Scallop gripped the rail and looked overboard, reaching for a paddle to swipe at Skate as he mischievously flew from beneath the boat, Leaf has previously told him the tale several times over.

🌿

THEY BEACHED THE SKIFF ON a short stretch of sand between twisted mangroves, pulling it as far inland as possible. Though slavers could not make water this shallow, pirates were an ever-present threat to the middle keys. There would be no fire tonight.

High ground displayed the ruins of a building. Barely.

The structural remnants were filled with spindly palmettos; walls crumbled into the soil that fed the tree roots, further fracturing the foundation.

The boys scouted the island. Scallop waded out to a nearby shoal to spear crabs. Hardy broke off a palm frond and fervently swept away several inches of sand until they could discern a worn tile floor. Sea roaches scurried while mosquitoes swarmed in the dust. Leaf wondered if the story of the Lamprey children served as a kind of border: salts south of the middle keys were wary of the dangers of Canal City and had a bedtime story with which to instill caution before more corporeal sharks gnawed the bottoms of their children's fragile rafts. Yet here were the boys, camping on the demarcation line. From here on out, the winds would blow them in strange ways. Light faded. Leaf asked Hardy what he knew about the fall of Miami and Canal City's rise.

"It's dirty and dangerous, and the dive boys there are real sharks, we but minnows in their mouths unless we walk knives out."

His speech reverted to the bravado of Marathon slang: posture and ceaseless activity to sweep away impending darkness.

"Well, only old salts call it Miami anymore. The people who live and die there call it Canal City, as that's all that's left: flooded streets between the broken hotels, the burned-out mansions and fallen bridges, and the crazies and fishermen who squat in such rubble."

Hardy paused and aimed an imaginary spear at some coconuts hanging from a nearby palm tree.

"Supposedly, folk from Marathon used to go there regularly before things got weird. Or weirder, I should say. Since the King Pelicans roosted, nobody goes north unless they leave to join the Kudzu Army. Or are taken by slavers."

He stopped and stretched, the palm frond bent over his shoulders, elbows over each end.

"See, the issue is water. Canal City gets its water from Okeechobee. The Kudzu Army keeps the lake clear, but the city is built on the backs of the slaves. There's a human aqueduct miles long. All these slaves passing water bucket by bucket, that's what makes the Pelicans kings. Cross a King Pelican and get sent to the line. Or worse."

Scallop entered the encampment and threw a netted knot of crab onto the sandy floor. He stood there, dripping, not knowing what action to take next that would keep his mind off their destination. Silence clung to them as both realized how exhausted they were. Dusk burnished further into night as they debated the dangers of building a cooking fire. Hardy asked Leaf if he wanted to go for a swim. The sky was deep blue; night's sail billowed at the ocean's edge.

"Hardy, I fall asleep immediately. I mean, the minute the sun goes down, I'm out. You couldn't wake me up if you wanted to."

He laughed, "Yeah, I'm the same after diving all day and then a night o' rum. One time I—"

"No, Hardy, it's different for me. Without the sun or any light, I just shut down. I'm out. For good."

"I understand." Tossing the palm frond, he laughed ruefully.

"Actually, I don't understand anything, Leaf. We're going to Canal City. You're telling me you're going to sleep like the dead on this island that no one would ever dare spend the night." He stalked about and rummaged through their supplies until he found a bottle of rum. Against the far wall, a lizard perched atop a corroded electrical socket. Leaf wavered.

"Ask Scallop...." he muttered weakly.

Never had Leaf tried to hang on to consciousness so long. He closed his eyes and tried to open them again, but the heaviness of twilight blew over him like shifting sand, compounding into a desolate dune, burying him under the cool granules of night.

LEAF NEVER WOKE DURING THE night and never dreamed. But having previously tasted the night, something in his being craved more. The full moon bathed him in its frail, wan light and his eyes involuntarily fluttered open. He examined the moon, running over its wise scars and mountainous contusions. Nearby the boys laughed, and Leaf smelled ginger beer. An empty bottle rolled across the sand-covered tile and landed against the sole of his foot. Out of the blue darkness, their entwined feet pushed against the sand. Moonlight painted their thighs the hue and stripe of lunar tigers. Scallop growled satisfaction; Hardy's elbow thrust in and out of the shadows; Scallop fingered his own chest and reclined farther into darkness. Leaf closed his eyes and listened to the softer sounds of the surf as the boys added a rhythm of their own.

The gravity of sleep tugged at him. As he drifted off beneath the stars, Leaf charted the knowledge and experiences he had gained and thought celestial thoughts. Maybe Hardy had a comet's heart and was drawn toward the nearest body. Scallop possessed the heart of a moon, distant but still luminous. If Leaf was what he ate, then his was a heart of suns, nourishing to all but potentially scorching. He had forgotten about Skate and worried that these new friends were eclipsing his first.

Was Skate an asteroid, tumbling through the solar surf, unable to draw others into his orbit? Leaf rolled over as the shadowy figure of one of the boys rose and stumbled off to retch between the pines.

LEAF AWOKE IMMEDIATELY AT THE first light of dawn. Low tide.

He walked the beach until he found Skate. Leaf passed his hand over Skate's back and felt him ripple in trepidation. When Skate rolled his eyes northward, Leaf nodded.

Scallop raced past them and dove in the water. Washing, he looked past Leaf as Hardy emerged from the overgrowth, scratching his stomach and rubbing his eyes. Hardy touched Leaf's shoulder as he passed and squatted in the surf. He scrubbed his belly, sniffed at his armpits, and then washed them, too. Skate jetted between his feet, furiously back-pedaled, eyes wild as the immediate water around Hardy yellowed. Hardy let out a sharp laugh and fell backward. Leaf stepped into the surf, more sure of himself and the water, having swum in Marathon, and stood behind Hardy to examine his back. A tiny barnacle clung to the corner of a scale that accented his spine—its purplish pucker whitened to a jagged edge. As he picked at it, Leaf thought of dormant volcanoes on the moon, But the barnacle refused to budge.

Scallop sloshed ashore. "Let's go. We can eat after we make sail."

Leaf and Hardy poured into the boat after Scallop pushed it free from the sand. They crested small waves, and soon Vampire Key disappeared behind them. The boys shared bread and oranges while Leaf sat low in the bow and watched for boats or a rise in the sea floor. Skate rode their wake for a while before adhering to the hull, a vigilant, living figurehead. Leaf enjoyed the sun. Quick shadows disturbed his light.

"King Pelicans," he whispered.

Hardy straightened and rearranged his tackle. Threading a hook, he said, "No worries, those are Brown Pelicans." The large birds flapped their wings intermittently above, coasting low over the ocean.

He cut bait. Separating a minnow's silver head from its body, he diced the length into even chunks. "You can just tell. Though if you're close enough to one to see its hand, you know you're in trouble."

Hardy stood, ready to cast line. "They take certain folk to their roost, the Aerie, supposed to be the tallest building left standing in Canal City. It's their castle, made of bone and bird shit. And Canal City is their town. They can see everything from there. But like I said—when you see one up close, it's coming for you."

He threw the fishing line as far as he could and hook, and all disappeared beneath the waves.

❦

SCALLOP PULLED UP THE TILLER as the boat slid over a shallow area.

An ancient storm-battered airport control tower rose out of the currents, metallic and listing, its roof thatched; fishing lines flowed out of its dark windows. They tacked to avoid it, and as the water deepened, they passed over the massive shadow of a sunken plane, like a silent, submarine albatross, wings extended expectantly. Schools of silver fish flashed through its rusting ribs.

They turned toward open water. Dark waves broke. The boys shared a jug of water and bits of stale bread but barely spoke.

Hardy gave up on fishing and napped in the bow, arm shielding his eyes, mouth open, snoring comical and steady. Scallop let Leaf take the tiller as the sail popped and snapped in the harsh wind. He taught Leaf how to keep the boat from tipping over, to face the waves and keep them to his back—he talked about how to right a capsized boat. Scallop was quick and clear in his instructions; the unspoken thought was that they might not all escape the dangers of Canal City and its masters.

SHALLOW MOON

GRAY GULLS DIPPED AND ROSE in the wind without flapping their wings. The boys spotted several fishing boats as Scallop dropped sail. The broken skyline of Canal City smoldered. Leaf had never seen tall buildings before and rode the bow to better scrutinize the wrecked structures: rooftop smoke from cooking fires gave the submerged city the look of permanent war. Laundry hung between former hotels tenanted by pirates and prostitutes.

Ragged, tall palms stretched over a beach of concrete fragments and upturned slabs of asphalt bejeweled with barnacles, slimy seaweed, and gaping fishheads.

"We'll wait until the fishermen head to shore and follow them in."

Hardy grunted in agreement, stretched, and yawned, having slept most of the day. Scallop dove overboard to cool off and quickly scrambled back on board. Restless, Hardy then swam with Skate. They splashed and lunged toward each other in mock attack. The sun pulled toward the horizon, and the first of the boats began to gather up their nets. Scallop waited until boats came from behind before hoisting sail. Boats by the hundreds aggravated the water like a swarm of mosquitoes.

Hardy pulled himself back into the boat. "We just can't slip in among the dive boys here. Canal City dive boys are all part of fierce gangs with specific territories," he warned.

"Constant skirmishes keep them from being a threat to pelican rule. If we make shore on the wrong turf, they'll make us wrestle the shark—stripped, given a knife, and forced to confront an angry shark herded into a tide pool."

The bowed wooden planks that linked the buildings of Canal City were heavy with one-armed and one-legged fisherman who had lost that fight. The boys decided to enter the city among the human muck and escaped slaves that scavenged the rubble of fallen buildings and hurricane debris that formed the jetties that reached out from the ruins like giant, hungry claws stirring murky waters.

Once again, Skate was made to guard the boat, though plaintive ripplings expressed his desire to go with them. His eyes pleaded. There were only a few hours of daylight left. Unsure of the safety of the boat or if Canal City would provide enough flittering light to keep Leaf conscious, they agreed to return at sunset and sleep in the skiff.

The surrounding fishermen dropped anchor and, wading ashore, gave a portion of their catch to a group of harbor boys on a raft, legs dangling in the water. Scallop followed, broke off a chunk of bread from their supplies, and gave it to the one who looked like he was the leader. He tore at it with filed-down teeth. Grunting approval, he shared it with the rest; each had tattooed lines dripping from their bottom lips down their chins, heads poorly shaved, what hair remained slathered with fish oil in the shark fin of a Mohawk. Black circles of sooty grease ringed dead eyes.

Leaf and his friends sloshed ashore. No one paid them any particular attention. Broken concrete formed the jetty populated with escaped slaves and feral children. An old man with leathery skin beat a limp octopus on a rock. Hungry children circled, hopeful a stray tentacle might break free and fly their way. Hardy strode confidently toward the rocks. Scallop was despondent—the journey had ended, and the search began.

He studied every face. The men and women who had escaped slavery all shared the same expression: something during their captivity had been stripped or burned away; they shuffled aimlessly, some stooping to foolishly drink the salt water. Scallop stared at their faces and understood that the man he was looking for might no longer resemble the father who raised him.

Hardy had scrambled up a rock, fishing spear between his teeth, and beckoned impatiently for Leaf and Scallop to follow.

Once atop the reef of wreckage, the boys could see how the ocean lapped at collapsed buildings in a shattered metropolis that rattled with parasitic life. Families gathered around roasting fish on rooftops; girls bathing in the canal squealed with glee as waves lifted them within reach of ogling boys leaning out windows.

Every remaining structure rang with an insane flurry of crying gulls. Those buildings reduced to rubble sprouted mangrove havens for crab and catchalls for refuse. Within these ruins, small palms wavered in the corners of exposed rooms. The boys stumbled down the other side of the jetty and sloshed through the shallow water of Ocean Boulevard. The scents of unfamiliar meat cooking over an open flame mingled with incense intoxicated Hardy and tore Scallop from his task. Leaf followed, sensing a futile labyrinth wherein those who struggled to keep from getting lost forgot that they had already drowned.

Buildings were linked by splintered planks and swaths of rubble; wooden bridges arched over the canals to allow small boats to flow underneath. Entire blocks had been filled with sand and detritus to form elevated open-air markets. Lean-to taverns operated next to barbers, blacksmiths, and various merchants.

Women swirled masses of shrimp and strange vegetables in ancient oil drums licked by fire. Tattoo artists bled symbols into the bare backs of boys. Beggars at every turn groped and pleaded. The sad question mark of a naked, dead child collected flies in one corner.

They walked slowly. Scallop searched faces. Hardy breathed deeply and exaggeratedly projected his strength. He was challenged by the atmosphere and hated being the alien, the rube. Scallop absently reached for Leaf's hand as a large, flat boat pushed down Ocean Boulevard. The passengers were mostly men, many of them black from the sun, docile from dehydration; he strained to see everyone on board. The boat was headed north: new conscripts for the human aqueduct. He opened his mouth to call out his father's name but paused—to do so would draw attention. Before that barge, another one, and behind it as before, a floating train of human desperation stretched in both directions. As he slowly closed his mouth and looked away, his grip on Leaf's hand slackened, and Leaf knew that he was giving up. His father had drowned or been killed or was a slave, and three boys in a violent urban wilderness could not save him. The breeze shifted, and rich smoke from one of the oil drums cut the air between them. He dropped Leaf's hand, and when the air cleared was gone. Leaf turned toward Hardy, but he was nowhere to be found.

Alone, Leaf took in the smells: fetid fruit, sewage, flesh. Smoke wafted through the air. And tension, a constant animal anxiety, rose and fell, relaxed by alcohol and narcotic smoke, creating a lull that invited attack and rape and reprisal, necessitating more apprehension. This was a city of appetite and knives. Strong, ropey fishermen still wet from the surf, their catches dying on their shoulders, eyed Leaf with speculation but assumed that he must already be claimed. Dive boys pushed past as Leaf looked for his friends.

One pirate stopped and stared. He let a plump reef shark slip from his shoulder as he approached. Constant work had kept his body young though he was an older man, and the sun had burned hard black coins into his bunched shoulders; white ribbons of scar tissue slashed brown forearms, and gaudy silver rings punctuated twisted fingers. He looked at Leaf with one blue, cataract-smeared eye, his other eye socket a dark hollow. Thinning hair was pulled down across his forehead to absurdly disguise the loss, weighted with a chunk of turquoise that failed to match his surviving eye in symmetry and color. He reached for Leaf and smiled, revealing hazardous teeth as black and slimy as kelp.

"Do you cook?"

"I don't even eat."

"You'll eat what I feed you." He laughed, and a shudder of rotten breath poisoned the air. His grip on Leaf's arm tightened as he spun the green boy around. His single eye rolled up Leaf's thighs and tried to pry his buttocks apart.

"You are a fine catch tonighty—we'll room under the moon and knock about like blind horseshoe crabs drunk on sea foam."

He grabbed Leaf's other arm and pulled him close—Leaf felt the man's growing excitement lift his oily loincloth, and he strained against his captor, calling out to his friends. The reef shark thrashed at their feet, its opal eyes fogged with death. The grinning pirate started to speak but stopped, his eye quaking back and forth as he released Leaf. He spun madly, groping for the machete protruding from the small of his back.

Hardy stood, breathing heavily, every muscle in his body tensed.

His head was freshly shaved. Only a blond flare remained: a harsh stripe down the middle. Each ear had been pierced. Faded cherry flamingo feathers brushed his shoulders. The dying pirate dropped on top of the reef shark, and his weight propelled the suffering animal across the bridge, over the side, and it was gone with a splash.

Blood pooled at Leaf's feet. Hardy had traded the fishing spear for a machete. He stepped onto the pirate's shoulder and pulled out the blade, cleaning it on the dead man's buttocks. Leaf stared; blood filled the space between his sandy toes, so he took a step backward. The crowd that had gathered began to disperse.

Bedraggled urchins rushed forward and pulled the earrings from the old man's ears, the rings off his fingers. A grumbling, obese shopkeeper approached with a large push broom to roll the corpse into the canal. Hardy grabbed Leaf's arm with the same force as the pirate had and steered him away.

"I'm sorry I left you, Leaf," he whispered. His grip softened. He let go and draped a welcome arm over Leaf's shoulder; his heartbeat resounded through his body. Leaf's heart beat quickly, too. He planted his feet on the planks.

"We have to find Scallop."

But Scallop found them and quickly looked from Hardy's wild haircut to the new machete vibrating in his hand and walked past them, whispering, "Keep moving. I heard people talking about us, calling us 'minnows,' and that's not good." Hardy scowled and looked up and down the crowded street, daring anyone to meet his angry gaze.

THEY CROSSED DANGEROUS BRIDGES THICK with loitering dive boys.

In several areas, trees had hooked their roots into the rubble of collapsed buildings and formed hamlets, shanty towns smoked with dinner fires and pulsed with arguing families and screaming children and laughing drunks. Hardy's transformation helped them blend in. He guided them through the throng as Scallop scanned every passerby and open storefront, his face expressionless.

The sun had begun to set.

A small brown-skinned naked boy, face and torso painted blue, approached with a shiny smile that would put a great white to shame.

"Need a room?"

He clenched and unclenched dirty palms as he spoke, a sign that he could be trusted.

The boys pushed past as he whispered, "Minnows don't last long, sleeping on the beach."

Hardy sneered over his shoulder, but Scallop turned and asked, "How much?"

"No jump. You just have to take the smoke in your arms. Try, try." His hands moved faster. Hardy shot them a look.

"He's in a cult. A cult of addicts and thieves."

The blue boy's eyes narrowed, and he bared sharp, metallic teeth. His gums were black from disease.

"See? Your smoke is burning your skull from the inside out."

Hardy menaced the boy with his machete. Brown spots of congealed blood flecked the blade. "Get away from us."

As the blue child slunk away, Hardy explained. "The barber warned me about them." He tapped the machete on his knee. It was nicked and cracked, with a handle that curved up to protect the hand of the wielder. Hardy tickled the feathers that hung from his ears. "These mean I am ready to fight and don't belong to a gang. And you two, you're nearly naked. Marathon people would assume you are dive boys, but here, without tattoos, you look like escaped slaves. Fresh meat."

Hardy was proud of his new knowledge. He was captivated by the dark energy that wove around the canals and bridges. The malignant mystery of the submerged city had gotten under his thick scales and festered with bubbling curiosity. He wanted to stay, not to explore but to conquer.

Defeat had enveloped Scallop. They would not find his father.

This was a city for orphans and pirates, and night was coming. Leaf thought of the White Flamingo's prophecies. Scallop denied his most meaningful catch and felt weak. The boys sensed he was tired and hurried toward a large, ruined hotel. Part-inn, mostly brothel, the hotel teemed with the wicked and the drugged.

Their jump bought them the rare room with a door. Leaf hoped that the boys would not open that door until dawn and knew he was wrong as his eyes fluttered and the sun turned away from the world in disgust.

SAND BAR

SUNLIGHT SPREAD FROM BENEATH THE curtain and slowly crawled up the prone form of Scallop, sleeping against the wall with Hardy's machete in his lap. The room was empty, with no furniture, walls scarred by fire, mildew, and insane graffiti. Leaf stood, pulled back the curtain he had assumed concealed a bathroom, and discovered a gaping hole overlooking the ocean. This particular corner of the hotel had fallen into the sea. Leaf could see outside and down into the room below and above. A steady stream of boats headed out to fish the sea. Gulls worried the pile of rock and broken brick below. Leaf stood and fed on sunshine. Waves crashed as a dank offal smell reached him and was in turn erased by the sharp salt of a strong ocean wind. The breeze subsided, and fragrant rot again permeated the room. An endless wind could scour the city, and it would never be clean.

Scallop scowled in his sleep. Leaf did not want to wake him, so he sunned himself at the edge of the floor, feet dangling into the room below. An infant cried. Curses rang out from the boardwalk.

Gulls screeched in unison; the alarmed birds banked as a whole, and the sky emptied. The people below took this as an obvious sign, and though they went about their business, all were somewhat cowed. A line of pelicans soon appeared, black against the cloudless sky. Leaf involuntarily shivered. He understood; these were King Pelicans. Larger than average, their ragged wings dripped shadow over the denizens of the canals.

They turned south and were soon small, tumorous specks on the horizon.

The gulls returned to annoy the makeshift docks and tattered rooftops. Leaf heard Scallop exhale. The machete slid from his lap and rattled on the dirty concrete floor. Awake, he stood and stretched and then squatted beside Leaf. Whatever had transpired the previous night took its toll on Scallop. He was listless and unresponsive. During breaks in the din of the city, the surf's sound asserted itself. Leaf felt the warmth of Scallop's body next to his, but only just so: Leaf thought of him as a sick moon, pulling at the tide of his thoughts, but with a degraded orbit. Scallop finally coughed and squeezed Leaf's knee.

"Let's go get some breakfast."

He didn't mention Hardy but hung the machete on the rusty shower head behind the curtain; the blade clanked against a cascade of broken tile above the breaking surf. Scallop noted the handwritten number on the door as he closed it behind them. The hall was thick with cooking smoke and the smell of frying fish and urine. The darkness frightened Leaf, and he clung to Scallop while urging him forward. The makeshift stairwell was outside the building, and they quickly made their way down.

Leaf again found the number of people shocking. A gang of children menacing the air with palm-frond swords raced past like skittish lizards.

Dive boys worked the crowd, slapping palms, gripping forearms in elaborate greeting, gritting teeth, and shaking their heads in mock-warrior moves. Tattoos gripped their shaved skulls like the talons of ferocious black birds. Women pulled or pushed infants, clucked at vendors, feigning disdain toward each other with their chins in the air. Scallop strained against the flow and pulled Leaf along; they raced across a rickety bridge as a ferryman shouted at the fishermen to pull up their lines as he navigated a squat barge below. He alternated sides with a long pole while a small, diligent girl raced from stern to bow with a large palm frond, fanning the flies and seagulls away from its cargo: a pile of corpses. Scallop noticed that Leaf was staring and whispered in his ear, "Fertilizer." He shuddered and quickened his pace. Leaf followed.

After buying some skewers of meat, they separated from the crowd and made their way to the end of a rocky jetty. Feet absently combing the water, Scallop noisily sucked the smoldering meat off the charred stick. Boats harried the horizon like gnats.

"I want to keep walking north."

Leaf nodded a silent consent, and they were off.

Leaf hoped that Scallop was not thinking about walking into the Everglades to find his father. They simply would not survive.

The glades were thick with alligators and snakes. Worse were the wild ones, the men and women who had turned their backs on speech and clothes and sanity to become savages, carnivores.

They would tear the boys apart. But as they walked, Leaf understood. As the crumble of buildings slowly ceased, large piles of trash guarded by feral children grew. These receded to barren beach. The sun rose, and the afternoon heat simmered. A few steely old solitary men stalked the shore for crab. This was what Scallop craved: a sky unmarred by smoke and the angry racket of too many people on too little land. They walked until they found the rise of a broken bridge ensnarled in a mangrove riot. The pass was shallow enough for them to cross. Sand-colored rays scooted out from under their feet, and Leaf thought fearfully of Skate.

The other shore was pristine. Vines of purple morning glories snaked across the sand. The beach was littered with palm fronds and bits of plastic, and worn boards. This much-uncollected firewood meant they had left Canal City far behind. Scallop visibly relaxed and stripped off his loincloth, playfully catching it with his foot and kicking it toward Leaf. As he caught it, Scallop did cartwheels in the surf. Water sparkled off his turns, and the spray refreshed Leaf's face. Clutching Scallop's loincloth, he laughed and chased after this new spirit.

They followed the winding strip of sand until it widened and rose. They ignored a broken stretch of road cracked with weeds and stuck close to shore. As they meandered up the beach, crabs pulled their sand-caked claws into freshly dug holes. Dunes rose, so they plundered them: rushing the sandy mounds with utter abandon until clunky pearls of sand streaked their skin, powdering thigh and elbow. The dunes deepened. The wind carried the sound of whistling and laughter within these soft canyons. They crouched. Still, they tried to discern the nearness of the source.

Scallop struggled back into his loincloth. They crept forward.

They observed a dark woman with wild hair tied back from the grassy crest of a mountainous dune. She was cleaning a fish in the middle of a small encampment. The center of the dunes had been naturally hollowed out. The family secreted within had added support with well-placed boards and carefully planted cattails. A simple hut, nothing more than a boat's preserved bow on stilts, provides shade for an infant in an oil-drum cradle.

Scallop elbowed Leaf's ribs and pointed with his chin: the indentation of an absent skiff was impressed onto the sand. Her mate had left to fish for the day. Leaf admired the simple tranquility of their humble hovel, an oasis far from the shadow of the pelicans, protected by the waves and creeping kudzu. They lived as people ought to live. Their private enclave reminded him of what he had left behind. He wondered if his house had fallen into the ocean, if coral filled the kitchen, if hammerheads lounged on the stairs. Surely by now, sand had filled the pool, and rising waves had smoothed the entire affair away, a forgotten mirror buried by the sea.

Though the woman's song had not changed, the whimsy of the tune had flattened into something false. She had noticed them and was pretending to go about her business. As she eyed the sleeping baby in the crib, she was really judging the distance and speed with which she could reach the spear beside it.

Leaf wanted to emerge from hiding, explain themselves, and make friends, but he knew they were trespassers to her. No matter what he said, she would see them as dive boys concealing sharp teeth with which to eat her child. Scallop had already begun inching back down. Ashamed, Leaf followed. They hung low until they had cleared the dunes. Scallop grabbed a stick and etched large, looping symbols into the hard sand close to the water. As he drew these lines, Leaf asked him what they meant.

"It's just my name. My Dad taught me how to write my name."

Leaf stared hard and long at the mysterious language until it, too, was carved into the wet shoal of his desire.

❧

CANAL CITY AT HIGH TIDE: rising waves returned all manner of boats to the devastated shore. Dive boys and fishermen returned with full nets, ready to trade their catch for rum, bread, or a favorite whore. The unlucky stayed out to fish deeper, longer, many to return empty-handed, hull loaded with bitterness and disappointment to fuel brawls and stabbings. The sudden throng annoyed the boys as they returned to the city. Leaf asked to check on Skate, but Scallop wanted to find Hardy first, and when they got to their room, he was passed out on the floor with two dive boys. Hardy was on his stomach; on his back, a new tattoo struggled to the surface beneath a slick smear of drying blood. One of the dive boys was naked, his legs splayed in a pool of his own urine. All three held empty rum bottles.

Scallop swore under his breath and rolled Hardy over with his foot. Hardy's face was bruised from fighting. Scallop searched his shorts for jump and found too many coins, more than they had arrived with. He counted out a meager amount for himself and returned the rest.

"Stay here. I'm going out for food." Leaf wanted to protest, but through the curtain, he could see that the light outside was growing dim. He settled down as far from the boys as the room permitted and held the curtain aside to watch the ocean. Boats made for shore. Electricity flickered to life in certain buildings.

&

BELOW, OBLIVIOUS DARK SURF CRASHED. Sunlight faded, and Leaf started to doze. The curtain fell. Shrouded in darkness, he heard the two dive boys stir.

One groggily whispered. "Hey, this must be the boy Hardy was talking about."

Leaf blinked and struggled to keep his eyes open.

The other slurred, "Yeah, yeah, and he's greener than sawgrass."

A bottle rolled across the floor. Hardy snored.

"Eh, do you believe what he said about the boy's magic spout? Wanna take a long drink?"

Rough fingers crawled up Leaf's thigh. He tried to tighten his protective leaf against tugging hands. One dive boy moved atop him, blotting out the remaining light in the room, and Leaf ceased to struggle against the inevitable night.

SMOKE

LEAF WOKE UNDER A HEAVY weight. A dive boy was passed out on top of him. Face to face, his breath fetid with alcohol and dank from tooth decay. Leaf pushed the dive boy off; he was young, boney, and filthy. With ankles a haze of tattoos, he was missing all of the toes on his right foot. Woozy from the lack of light, Leaf pulled back the curtain. Scallop squatted over the opening, vomiting a pinkish sludge into the sea below. His complexion was pallid and weak. He looked at Leaf, but his eyes were unfocused. He tried to say something, but more vomit rose.

Leaf fed from the dawn and stood resolute by his side, a palm tree centuries old and used to storms. Scallop meekly gripped his legs for support. A dark woman with a baby kept looking up at them from the floor below, angry at the early morning disturbance.

Leaf flourished in the light and turned slowly. With his back to the sun and sea, he felt a liquid cooling on his inner thighs.

He patted himself and came away with a sticky substance on his fingers. A viscous mixture of rum and semen painted his butt.

In the main room, Hardy was sprawled in a corner. His scales seemed to have thickened and widened as if their few days in Canal City had incited new, reptilian growth. Leaf yearned for the family secreted in the dunes. He wished for clean, crystalline sand forming soft, warm walls, shifting protection against the world, a personal desert on the edge of a protective sea. Anything but this.

Scallop threw up again. The woman below banged on the ceiling with the blunt end of a fishing spear while Leaf fixed the curtain to block out a maximum amount of sunlight. He absently pulled at the leaves that ringed his neck and discovered his shark's tooth necklace was missing. Frantically, he searched the room. Rolling dive boys over, rifling dirty pockets, he could not find it. Clouds passed. Darkness settled back into the room as he curled against Hardy's brick hide and slept again.

EYES OPEN. A HAZE OF smoke had settled near the floor. Kneecaps and bottles broke through the fog. Surreptitious discussion, rude whispers. Eyes closed.

NOISE. LEAF PULLED UP BY unknown arms. A party. Dive boys and off-duty hookers. Someone had brought a music machine: a silver box broken and repaired many times over that squeaked and sputtered metallic drum beats. A bottle was brought to his mouth, and he drank wine. His throat constricted around effluvial acid. Boys laughed, and Leaf searched the room for Hardy and Scallop, wondering if he might not have somehow woken up in a different building. But no, the woman from downstairs was squatting in the corner, her dress up above her knees, exposing a hairy vagina stuffed with a stained-brown rag. She drank from a plastic jug and looked annoyed, aroused, and bored all at once. Boys laughed, and Leaf saw Scallop weaving toward him.

His smile was unhooked, eyes rheumy with alcohol. He brought a bottle to Leaf's lips, and timidly, Leaf drank. Surprise. Not wine, mostly water with a smooth, milky additive. He dropped the bottle, but a dive boy reverentially caught it before it hit the filthy floor. Leaf smacked his lips, astonished to have tasted himself.

Leaf peered closely at Scallop but could not find him inside a vacant, dirt-smeared face. Scallop grinned through insipidly, puffy crocodile lips coated white around the edges. More people pushed into the room, but Hardy was not among them.

New dive boys crowded around Leaf. The youngest, bucktoothed and playful, with a mess of dirty blond hair and hopeful eyes, looked up at him and talked as if they'd conversed before.

A constellation of dark pimples crusted his cheeks, liverish rubies of sincere infection. His fingers played around Leaf's waist. They held hands. He reminded Leaf that his name was Gourd, quietly desperate for Leaf to remember; his eyes watered when he realized that Leaf did not. Another bottle of rum was passed around.

The woman from downstairs lit a fat cigar as Leaf wondered who was watching the baby.

❦

THE CURTAIN TACKED OVER THE gaping hole in the hotel room wall trapped stale smoke and rank breath. Leaf reached for the thin stream of sunlight that cut like a laser through a slit in the cloth. Gourd groaned at his side and reached out for him, but Leaf shook him off and, pushing past bodies, settled before this slender ray and allowed it to burrow into his pores. Sunlight painted a perfect line down the middle of his face, delineating two dark halves forever ready to reunite. Legs crossed, he sat and tried to draw as much energy as possible. He needed to clear his mind to help Scallop clear his. He didn't want to turn his head and look for his friend, though; the meridian of light felt so balancing that Leaf worried he would lose it if he moved, the world would plunge into permanent darkness, and all the boys would rise up from the floor, nocturnal sharks hungry for his flower, and feast on his body. Or had that already happened? As the line of light shifted, he followed—a monkish, forlorn sunflower. Turning, he found Scallop pressed to the floor beneath a fat, dozing prostitute. A stray nipple had popped out of her costume, an elaborate system of black string that cut into her flesh like netted jellyfish. The breast hung near Scallop's open, snoring mouth like an over-ripe avocado.

Strength renewed, Leaf reached for the curtain, about to tear it away from the window, bathe himself in light, banish all shadows, and cleanse the room when Hardy kicked open the door. New tattoos slashed arms loaded with bottles, and dual machetes slapped at his thighs. A herd of dive boys with alert, hungry eyes surged at his shoulders. Too many boys. Leaf sought to escape. The sheet at the bathroom doorway fluttered slightly, and he wondered how far the drop—if he would survive the plunge into the cool, clarifying water.

With a forced cheer, Hardy woke the room, poured rum into sleeping mouths, and shouted for someone to pull the cord on the music machine, but always with an eye on Leaf. Once the boys were roused and the party in full swing, he took Leaf in his arms. Leaf squirmed against the clammy warmth of Hardy's hands, the tiled muscle of his chest. Hardy whispered, cajoled, uncorked a bottle, and forced Leaf's lips apart. He pushed the bottle against clenched teeth, and rum leaked at the corner of Leaf's mouth, but most of it wormed its way down his throat. Hardy's black pupils dilated as his captive's soft hands forded his lap and dug into his shorts to pull on thickening flesh.

More rum flooded Leaf's gasping mouth. Reason eclipsed with a brutal kiss, scaly hand over his eyes a tide of permanent night, dark water filled with dive boys, knives between their teeth, plunging toward a shifting ocean floor of silvery silt that promised gold coin. He swam after them, deeper and deeper until it was impossible to ever return to the surface again.

WELL AFTER MIDNIGHT, THE ROOM had grown morose. A recently stabbed dive boy sulked by the door. His tearful lover absently tended to the dark wound while eying potential replacements against the far wall. Leaf was awake again, barely, as the break in the wall had been uncovered and weak moonlight fed him.

He tried to turn toward the poor illumination but could not move. Beneath the window, Scallop slouched though his lap pooled with recent vomit. A cloud crossed the moon, and Leaf faded. Hardy and two dive boys lurched toward him. Hardy whispered, and the red-eyed dive boys sneered and nodded in rapid agreement.

They dropped their shorts and took aim. Hardy roared, and Leaf willed himself toward darkness as the dive boys drunkenly watered their plant.

A DIFFERENT ROOM. NO WINDOWS. Utter blackness. It smelled of feces, spilled liquor, hopeless semen, and dissipated smoke.

The cold concrete floor was carpeted with dirty dive boys. Leaf blinked as the door opened and light filtered in. Somewhere Hardy whispered. Leaf realized the danger they were all in: his entire being exuded oxygen during the day, releasing carbon dioxide during the night. Without knowing it or meaning to, he steadily wove a cocoon of death—he could suffocate an entire room in his sleep. He wanted to warn everyone and struggled to maintain consciousness as the door closed.

Gourd, limp and sticky, was pasted to his thigh. Leaf heard Hardy's whisper rise to a threat. The boy he was bargaining with backed down. Jump was exchanged, and Leaf felt a towel being unwrapped from around his waist; he realized he was gagged.

He tried to raise his hands to his face but could not. They were tied behind his back. Below, he sensed kneeling shadows and heard nervous laughter. Rough teeth ground his stem. Someone pulled Gourd off his thigh, and the dive boy woke and angrily struck out at the aggressors. They swiftly beat him into submission. Strong hands grasped Leaf's buttocks. More boys roused and piled on, and the room grew heated with their erotic ministrations. Soon after, his litter of addicts slumped away, quiet and content at his feet. The door opened again, and the drowsiest dive boys were taken away as more acolytes rushed in.

L I G H T N E S S

SOMEONE ACCIDENTALLY OPENS A WINDOW and.

I.

Return.

To my sun.

Unimaginable waves, waves I cannot describe, reach me. I again understand the bend of space, the undulation of the cold, celestial ocean forever flowing with indiscriminate light; the light that reaches you or not, light that paints Pluto or moves on and strikes an object several million years later or not. But light always lands; it never dissipates. It just comes and comes and comes.

Like me.

I am no longer tied up but sit on a ridiculous throne bejeweled with coral and shell and a marvelous fan of radiant palm fronds.

Maybe what I have been doing here is not so wrong.
Not one of my worshipers has been hurt.
I certainly feel no pain.
Has anyone checked on Skate?
The thought of my first friend sets my mind spinning.
This is a different room than before. We are at sea level. I
hear waves crashing nearby. Thick mold runs up the walls in
wicked flames of black crust.
Where is Scallop?
I am not doing anything wrong.
I am not doing anything at all.
Pollination happens.
Oh, Skate.
The window closes. Murmurs from the disturbed. A cough.
But the light never completely dissipates.

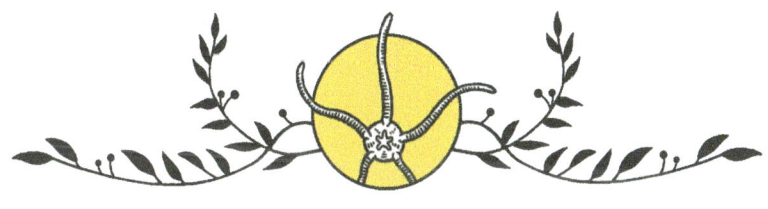

PRIVATE
DUNES

FURIOUSLY BLINDING SUN FILLED LEAF, who expanded like an ecstatic puffer fish. Delirious, he wondered if he might actually be floating. A sublime dawn of soft blues and canary yellows slowly swept over broken buildings.

He felt as if he were levitating, as if he rested on a cloud streaming down a rickety path, a pinwheel of quiet buildings and palms turning past. And the sun just kept finding him. In between the shadow of every building, it shone through, piercing him with loving, healing arrows of light. Leaf must have laughed because Scallop whispered, "Quiet, we're not off the reef yet."

Leaf turned to tell him that he had, in fact, never seen a reef but had always wanted to but was instantly sobered by the sight of him.

Scallop was fearful and ashen, breath ragged. Gaunt cheekbones framed torn burned lips. His arms were scarred, his ribs showed, and bruises covered his body.

He was missing an ear.

"Oh, my Scallop." Leaf wanted to give him his light and tried to reach for him, but his left arm would not obey.

Part of Leaf's chest and arm, up to the elbow, had darkened with thorns. He ran a green hand across this oaken casing. The barbs were twisted and blunt. His skin is now tougher than Hardy's.

Somehow Scallop had stolen Leaf away and into a wheelbarrow. Leaf's green feet bobbed as the wheelbarrow bounded down the wobbly lane of boards and packed earth. His toes were black with grime, glued together with the viscous seed and rum of worshiping dive boys. His pitiable stem flopped up and down with his legs splayed, and the tip gnawed to an uneven stump. Leaf concentrated on the sun and willed this part of himself to mend.

He ached for rainwater and the opportunity to inspect Scallop, to walk with him into the sea and hold him below the violent waves until all this had washed away.

Scallop wheeled him down several blocks; one of Hardy's machetes was tied around his waist. They crossed treacherous bridges and chose back alleys as fishermen loaded their skiffs.

The boys expertly avoided the noxious splash from buckets of filthy water emptied from high windows. Scallop coughed out phlegm. Renewed blood coursed through Leaf's veins, cleansing him. The farther away they were from the permanent night of abandoned hotels and constant smoke, the better he felt. Leaf thought Scallop was panting from exertion but realized he was whispering, over and over, "I'm so sorry, I'm so sorry."

Leaf shifted in an attempt to look over his shoulder and tell him that it was okay, that he owed no apologies, but he almost turned the wheelbarrow over in doing so, so he stilled and let the journey happen.

A proud fisherman strode past, a tower of refined muscle and scar, with a long bamboo pole balanced on his shoulders. He did not even look as they passed; his permanent squint was focused solely on the sea, measuring the outgoing tide, and Leaf realized then that Scallop was not apologizing to him but to his father.

Above, tall spindly palms bounced in the breeze. Beyond the rolling clouds, the black silhouette of a lone pelican kept pace with their progress.

ON CANAL CITY'S OUTSKIRTS, LEAF could calm Scallop and convince him that he was well enough to walk. They sold the wheelbarrow to a delighted family of coconut harvesters for enough jump to buy fruit and meat skewers and even a clutch of boiled eggs. Then they walked in silence. They passed the devastated bridge that had marked the end of their last excursion and soldiered on. They walked until Canal City was no longer visible and came to rest on a virgin stretch of sand. Scallop bathed in the sea. He scrubbed his underarms, wrung out his loincloth, and somberly endured the pain of salt water cauterizing his many wounds. Small burns twisted across his back and his hands. If a boat passed, he paused to solemnly follow its progress, more out of habit than hope. Up and down the beach, small waves gently kneaded masses of seaweed spackled with bits of broken shell.

Spent, Scallop slept on his back.

While Scallop rested, Leaf took the machete and slit the tip of his green finger, and circled the ragged hole of Scallop's missing ear with his blood. He gently blew on the coagulating viscous sap until it solidified into thick emerald amber. The cut began to percolate. Leaf teethed on the tip of his finger lest the wound close. More green blood flowed out.

He painted the burns and cuts which pocked Scallop's body and wished he could excrete an ointment to soothe the young man's scarred heart. Scallop exhaled and relaxed further into a deep sleep, working his jaw in silent agonies and arguments.

LEAF PICKED AT THE THORNS that rode his shoulder and arm. He wanted to peel them off and let new flesh flourish under the afternoon sun but remembered the roaming tree of hands. He wondered if it was prowling the ocean floor and shuddered, imagining that it had developed a shark-like mouth of briars in the center of each palm, indiscriminately grinding fish and swimming children into chum. He decided to wait until dusk and goad Scallop into building a fire so he could throw his thorns into the flame.

AFTER WAKING, SCALLOP SMILED SHEEPISHLY and fingered the newly minted ear, white as a shell, clinging to his cranium.

"It's itchy."

He stretched and yawned and slapped at his stomach. Standing, he attempted a back flip and promptly landed on his ass.

They laughed, and Leaf helped him stand and dusted the sand off Scallop's muscular legs. They waded through cattails bobbing in the wind and found an abandoned, roofless hut to squat in for the night. Scallop broke off a sturdy palm frond, swept the sandy floor smooth, and uncovered a rusty spool of useable fishing line. Leaf gathered driftwood, hoping it would not be enough, that Scallop would need him to stay warm at night.

Scallop caught crabs. They cut more palm fronds, wove them into tight bowls, and put them in the corners of their makeshift encampment to catch next morning's dew. Scallop patiently tried to set a patch of Spanish moss on fire to cook the crabs. He was amazed by his recovery and couldn't stop fingering his new ear. He looked renewed, alive, and in the excitement, tumbled through the surf shouting his joy. Later, while he fished off the posts of a disintegrated pier, Leaf sat by the fire, pulled off the bark and thorns that riddled his side, and shoved the pieces into the glowing embers. Dark flesh curled and popped in the flames. Scallop's shadow interrupted this sacrifice; he presented Leaf with a fantastic silver fish. Leaf smiled sheepishly, and Scallop smacked his forehead, and both laughed—in a rush to thank Leaf for restoring his ear Scallop had forgotten that he only ate sunshine.

He shook the sand off a piece of driftwood and laid the fish out. He cleaved the head off the fish with a whack from his machete, cut pieces of meat, and ate them raw. In the distance, a slaver ship smoked.

"Hardy sold our boat the very first day." He wiped his mouth on the back of his hand. "I tried to stop him, but he convinced me that if we got rid of the boat there'd be no turning back; we couldn't stop looking for my father even if we wanted to."

Leaf sat up and put his hand on Scallop's shoulder.

"He said he sent Skate home, and I wanted to believe him, but—" And Scallop cried.

"I just didn't know what to do, and then the dive boys started feeding off of you like minnows, and Hardy poured rum into me every minute of the day. But I can't blame him for that, Leaf; if he didn't offer a bottle soon enough, I'd snatch it out of his hand."

He shot Leaf a dark look.

"I kept thinking about what the White Flamingo said—that I was destined to fail. I just wanted to be numb. Hardy was swinging, though, having the time of his life! Jump flowed as he sold you off, but I never took a taste, Leaf, not once. I didn't stop the others, though, and I should have. I should have."

Knees drawn up to his chest, arms locked, Scallop started to cry harder. Leaf spoke: "Scallop."

"No, I took you out of there for selfish reasons, Leaf, and not my ear. Would you believe it didn't hurt? Not more than a headache, really, I was so rummed. No, I heard some dirty dive boy and Hardy conspiring. See, the dive boy's father had grown pineapples, so this nasty little rotten fish told Hardy he'd help quadruple his profit. All they had to do was dice you up and plant the parts."

Scallop swallowed and stared into the sand. He dug canals of regret into the white earth with his heels. "And that's when I snapped out of it, Leaf. I wasn't about to let them parcel you out like a damned coconut vendor, so I stole that wheelbarrow, and here we are." The last words whispered, and a mirthless laugh; the new ear glowed red hot with shame. "And, and. Leaf. Since full moon on Marathon, I wanted you to myself."

Leaf felt his eyelashes grow: reaching, yearning, stretching, black vines aquiver. A tiny carnation budded and unfolded over his heart.

They both wept, and Scallop's lament salted his cheeks and stung his eyes red. Leaf gathered him in his arms; Scallop resisted, but Leaf pulled him up with a strength that surprised them both. They walked to the surf, and Leaf pushed him into the rolling waves and baptized him with kisses. Scallop enfolded Leaf in his arms. They hungrily teethed on one another's tongues.

Callused hands gripped Leaf's shoulders as Scallop shimmied out of his loincloth. He kicked it to the shore and stood above Leaf, legs apart. The curvature of his thighs possessed a muscular complexity. Leaf's hands anchored Scallop's feet as Scallop pulled Leaf's head into his lap.

Scallop sighed. Leaf found that Scallop tasted like the clean bitterness of seawater during a cold and heavy rain. They dropped back into the loam of the crashing surf and became entangled like storm-tossed seaweed, ragged and weary, uprooted but sovereign, floating free and alive.

🍃

AN AFTERNOON NUDE IN THE dirty spume of spent waves, legs entwined, arms out, fingers sunk into the sand. That immortal moment when the sun stops but the wind keeps coming, spinning lovers up into the air—a cocoon of clouds and breath—and every look creates a new language neatly understood by the other. A closeness so compact each whisper becomes a shout, every kiss volcanic. As Scallop rested, Leaf fingered the tip of his own stamen and lightly painted each of Scallop's scars with emerald honey. Little green suns sank into his flesh and dissipated. Scallop would take a while to regain his weight, but as his skin healed, he looked more like himself and less a rattled shade from the city.

Scallop snored. Leaf traced his ribs and outlined the coin of his distended belly button. The flesh at his elbows bunched like excess netting. The sudden hair that gathered below his waist looked oily but was incredibly soft. Here Leaf sifted out bits of sand and shell as Scallop gained girth in approval. Permanent scars marched down his legs. Leaf could not repair these and did not want to; they marked encounters with reefs and fishhooks that proved that the world had carved him into a man. Scallop's pearl ear attested to his being permanently changed yet changeable.

Leaf examined his own flesh. Every wound he had ever suffered had gone green. He looked the same as when he was on the island. Not quite. From the fingertip that he had first cut to heal Scallop, the probing bud of a sprightly vine sprouted. Disturbed, Leaf pulled it free. It writhed in his palm. As he brought his arm back to throw it into the sea, he paused, then popped the bud in his mouth and swallowed.

Leaf touched Scallop's toes, and Scallop reflexively dug his heels deeper into the damp sand. Scallop threw an arm across his eyes as his sleep grew restive. Chapped lips mouthed silent syllables of lamentation. His penis withdrew into its fleshly cloak like a disgruntled hermit crab. Leaf smoothed the surrounding sand, wishing to give him a bed of clouds.

MEDITATIVE BENEATH THE SUN, ABSORBING light, Leaf lengthened his torso and counted his ribs; the new flower above his heart had flourished and turned a surprising green to blend back into his flesh, giving his pectorals some much-needed heft. White spikes ringed Leaf's neck as the petals had begun to grow again like fledgling wings.

Scallop swam. His head bobbed on a distant wave, and the hair close to his scalp sparkled with beads of water. He waved and then dove and re-emerged, closer, bounding between the waves as naturally as a dolphin. He stepped out, water snaking across his skin in the strong breeze. He tossed a piece of sea glass toward Leaf, who, though his eyes were closed, felt its shadow cut across the sun and expertly caught it. Scallop whistled, impressed. Though crusted with sand, the large piece of azure sea glass was uniformly smooth. Years of tumbling in the tide had worn away the sharp edges and made it a small marvel. As he had so many times with Skate, Leaf turned toward the ocean and pitched it across the water. It skipped several times before sinking, another jewel lost to the depths that created it.

They had stayed the night in the little hut. Leaf had wrapped Scallop like a vine. Though the spot was secluded and comfortable, both boys thought it wise to put as much distance between them and Canal City as possible. They walked along the shore.

Large swaths of beach were clear from any sign that humanity had ever existed. Broken sand dollars filled their footprints. Thirsty, Scallop shimmied up a spindly palm tree and collected coconuts, breaking one on an outcropping of rock and greedily slurping up its wet innards. He took one of the baskets of palm fronds they had woven from the hut to carry the rest of the coconuts over his shoulder. The dunes, and the tranquil loneliness, reminded Leaf of his island, but he did not miss it. The island was now set in memory. A jewel, a fulcrum from which he swung farther and farther out; for the first time in his life, he possessed momentum and was curious to see what lay ahead. Scallop stayed by his side.

Occasionally he would look back to mark their progress. He had stopped tracking each and every boat, though when Leaf wasn't looking, he would watch the sky with concern.

The beach drifted inland for a bit and gave them two options: to travel toward the Everglades or northward, toward the ruins of Fort Lauderdale. The dangers of the vast swamp outweighed the nominal threats of a dead city, so they forded a shallow pass and resumed combing the beach. Large areas of Fort Lauderdale were poisonous marsh and lone, monolithic skyscrapers.

Only alligator trappers ventured there. Barren stretches of oil and chemical-saturated sands made for a no-man's-land, a good place to disappear.

They talked little, walked in one another's footsteps as they slid down dunes, and if a shift in the sand threw them together, they held hands for that moment. Water trapped by high tide carved out rivulets, and the boys splashed one another. Scallop tried to teach Leaf to cartwheel, but the green boy demurred. The beach expanded into a desert and a mountainous oasis arose with the broad swath of sand. The carcass of a collapsed condominium stretched across the dunes like so many giant, calcified dominoes. Long stripped of copper wire, glass, and any salvageable items of worth, residual innards extracted by storm surge, paint peeled away by relentless sun and hurricane, only an alien skeleton remained. Flora rode the upper tiers of its concrete spine, giving the bejungled dinosaur frame a velveteen sheen.

The gutted rooms possessed ecosystems particular to each crack and tumble of concrete: some were cubes of moss and lizard, others overflowed with coconut palms furry with banana spiders, and still, others offered exposed rusted steel rods, dead fingers breaking through this wild cornucopia as if grasping for even more.

Scallop whooped and hollered and declared this castle of rubble their new home. Climbing a jumble of concrete, he found a rough square space free of any undergrowth. Filled with fine sand, it provided perfect protection, shielding their presence from any passersby. Leaf was content to have Scallop make decisions and otherwise be preoccupied with happy activities. They gathered giant clam shells and made a fire pit in the center of their berth. Scallop sharpened a stick and stalked crabs near the shore. When he returned, he exclaimed that he'd never seen or caught as many large crabs before, and both felt safe and secure as if Canal City were a shared nightmare grown dim. Out of caution, Scallop kept the fire low, holding each other through the night.

FLIGHT

LEAF ABSENTLY STROKED THE PETALS, now fully regrown, at his neck and watched as Scallop stalked crabs in the distant surf. The paradisiacal days among the ruins gave them time to reflect and recover. Scallop talked about building a raft. They could drift south and find new islands. Sunlight poured over Leaf. Eyes closed, he sighed and renewed his concentration: his lungs had felt battered from their stay in the dank darkness of the shuttered rooms in Canal City. He channeled light into the arborous corners of his lungs and flushed out accumulating charcoal-like nodes of flesh. He sensed this good exercise and was pleased, though he wondered what else he could accomplish with his body with the right amount of attention and cultivation. A swift, momentary cloud blotted out the sun and was gone. The breeze picked up, and Leaf thought he heard Scallop shout something, but he was too far away. He lazily opened one eye and spied Scallop peeling away from the shore, fishing spear over his head, heading toward him at full speed. A flutter of shadows erupted in his peripheral vision, and Leaf stood up as all around him sand exploded.

Knocked on his back, winded, Leaf was aloft before he understood.

A dark quadrangle of wings closed above his head and momentarily blinded him. Sand poured out from beneath the net as it gathered around his frame, its squares cutting into his skin. As he rose, a lone King Pelican stood sentry, and they were eye to eye for a moment. The pelican was commander of the quartet above, rank distinguished by its Romanesque helmet.

A silver bullet gripped its skull and curled backward in a martial flourish. Militant slits displayed calculating eyes. It broke from Leaf's gaze to check the gigantic black watch low on its single human wrist. Leaf was so close that he noticed how well manicured its fingernails were, and then up he went. The King Pelicans above gained traction in the air and rose swiftly. Gigantic segments of the fallen building spread out below. Palms wavered. A coral snake sunned itself on an exposed ribbon of concrete. His concern for Scallop erased the marvel of flying above the earth. He was still a long way off from their hovel, though seeing Leaf netted in the sky did nothing to slow his determination. Leaf understood that they had come for him alone, that the inviting patch of sand he and Scallop had so naturally selected had been prepared for them.

The birds banked hard over the ocean. The utopian ruins were an illusion, a buried trap; they were heading toward Canal City, Scallop a shrinking, galloping speck on an expanding highway of sand. The helmeted pelican took flight and then the lead.

Leaf twisted and stretched as the ocean rippled below. The white crests of waves looked like tiny creases in a vast sheet. The pelican commandant flew close and eyed him until he stopped moving. A diagram of devastation emerged below: from beneath streaking sandbars and whitecaps, the grid of submerged blocks was visible. Buildings that had caved in on themselves were dark coral groves surrounded by sandy streets-turned-canals. And a crawling black wall. Leaf squinted at this strange formation: the human aqueduct which brought water to Canal City one bucket at a time, miles of sadness cutting toward the Everglades like a poorly stitched wound. The colors of the bay were visible, with darkened patterns of refuse and sewage. And slaver ships. Even from above, they were massive, evil trawlers for the damned. Then the dams and dry streets, soldiers from the Kudzu Army, the remnants of downtown Miami, and the eerie aerie, the towering center from which the King Pelicans ruled.

The pelicans swung their captor above the filthy white volcan that was the aerie. The headquarters of the *Miami Herald*, the formerly elegant Mediterranean Revival tower, was festooned with several tons of sun-baked bird shit. The stench that rose from the hellish castle was overpowering. The pelicans hovered over the cupola as grim slaves gathered their catch into waiting arms. Leaf was pulled from the net, and a rag was stuffed into his mouth. A slave put him over his shoulder like the day's catch before stooping before an opening molded into the guano. The slave then marched down a stairwell into the gloom of the pelican nest.

The gross odor of rotting fish and bird shit assailed Leaf. He had never felt such heat before, the humidity of fear. The slave's back slicked with sweat; Leaf struggled, hoping to wiggle free, but another slave, annoyed, approached with a black hood and bagged his head, and Leaf kicked, and more hands restrained him as consciousness faded to black.

BLACK CABLES TUNNELED IN AND out of thick white guano cracked like a desert floor. From beneath the lip of the hood, Leaf could see his feet planted in dark soil up to his ankles. He stood in a bucket of black dirt, hands tied behind his back to a wooden post. The earth was loaded with fertilizer, making him nauseous—he felt faint but heard voices. Several King Pelicans waddled into the room.

Bouncing on human hands, the pelicans were as ridiculous grounded as they were terrifying in flight. Leaf's hood was pulled off. Blinking, he saw that the room was circular and small, the crown of the nest. Each windowsill now held a bird and all avian eyes were on Leaf. Chemicals clouded his senses; queasy, he feared that the longer he remained planted, the more rooted he would become. He looked at the wires on the dung-covered floor and imagined himself an idiot vine nourished by bird shit, winding through the foul complex, stiff branches rising from his brow like antlers, a perch for pelicans. He craved a black eclipse. A permanent blot. Unfamiliar dry heaves shook his body. Leaf focused on the strange cranium of the nearest pelican; its scalp was stretched thin across its expanded dome. A tonsure of molted feathers gave this bird a more human appearance.

Another pelican leaped from its perch and approached. It glared at him through a pair of smudged reading glasses, a chain crusted with fish guts and feathers draped around its extended neck. With a quick flap, it mounted the base of the bucket and began to examine Leaf. Other members of the flock left their windowsills in turn. Nausea receded; fear demanded that he stay alert. With a practiced tilt, the pelican at his buried feet flicked its glasses from its bill. It shoveled its beak between his legs and tried to part his thighs. Mercifully, the ropes were tied too tight.

The perturbed pelican then snapped at the lone leaf protecting his stamen. It expertly clipped this acanthus and swallowed it whole.

Turning to the flock, it announced, "Dive boy salad!"

Gross-winged applause. Slaves led a chain of concubines into the room. The pelicans cackled and paraded about, beating their wings victoriously. Naked girls and painted dive boys squealed with fake laughter and wagged fish before the animated birds.

Leaf felt relieved to be dragged away.

A LOWER FLOOR WAS RESERVED for the menagerie, either collected or created, all caged—a prison of freaks. Two slaves dragged Leaf and his bucket down the corridor. They passed rows of cramped cells molded from chicken wire and packed mud and bird shit.

Silent creatures observed his arrival. Leaf was surprised to pass a crocodile kid. He recoiled, thinking it was Hardy, but the boy flashed a reptilian rack of jagged teeth, revealing a broad tail as he turned to follow Leaf's progress down the hall hungrily. Leaf's hopes were raised when he thought he spotted the White Flamingo. But as he neared her cage, he realized that the poor creature was indeed an actual bird, an example of pelican depravity, one whose features had been stretched into a mockery of a human face.

One cell was crowded with an unusual experiment. Skinny sad-eyed boys, all fitted with the webbed avian talons instead of hands, had hooked their hapless appendages in the cracked, chalky wire of their enclosure. Their mouths yellow beaks twisted in permanent smiles. Leaf was deposited into a cell. The stale air was thick with the dust of bird dung and the anxious sweat of other prisoners.

The next day he was watered and dutifully turned, so a different side of his body was exposed to the sunlight which poured through an open window. Days passed. Leaf wilted. Overwatered, he bent limply at his knees. His head was swollen while the petals fell from his neck. King

Pelicans waddled into his cell and questioned him. Still, the toxic fertilizer had so infiltrated his being that though his captors accused him of faking illness and menaced him with their snapping bills, they eventually relented and uprooted him from the bucket of black soil.

He sat before the window and pulled the sun into his body. He absorbed more light than necessary, sweating out the chemicals which clogged his blood and fouled his heart and mind. When he could stand, he was surprised that his cage door had not been locked. Wandering the hall, he noticed that most cages were left open. Some prisoners, like the crocodile kid, had to be restrained, but the rest were free to roam the building. The pelican boys had cornered the pseudo-White Flamingo in her cell while a member of their flock retrieved eggs from her nest. She shrieked in desperation as the boy awkwardly juggled eggs in his claw hands.

Leaf was thirsty and couldn't find water, so he braved the unguarded stairwell. The floor below was entirely given over to an assemblage of chugging generators, piles of salvaged parts, miscellaneous machinery, and oil drums. Cables flowed across the floor, into the walls, and out windows like black vines.

Stacks of old VCRs and rusted toasters, powdered with guano, lined the walls. Two King Pelicans played cards atop the centermost oil drum. They ignored Leaf, so he dipped a finger into one of the drums and was shocked to taste a sugary fuel. It burned his senses but was definitely vegetable in origin. The pelicans had stopped their game and regarded him with menace. One of them flicked his bill toward the door, and Leaf understood that he was meant to return to his cell.

LEAF SPENT HIS DAYS IN his cage, pulling the sunlight into his bones. Bored, he would take to the stairwell. Though barred from the roof and the ground floors, he was allowed to wander the tower halls. He discovered the hatchery by chance one day. The hatchery was a honeycomb of crates filled with eggs and electric lamps pasted to the wall with guano and duct tape.

The plush nests were fluffed with strips of dirty cloth and straw. The floor was strewn with bits of bone, broken eggshell, and yellow smears of gelatinous albumen and deflated yolk. The centrifugal nest was a tractor tire stuffed with more straw and shreds of old, faded newspaper.

A pelican with a pert powder-blue nurse's hat perched on her molted cranium sat atop a bevy of eggs. She stared down her bill at him. "Can I help you?"

It took him a full minute to respond; her voice was unnervingly human yet guttural as if a fish bone lodged in her trachea rode up and down her throat with every syllable.

"Why am I here?"

She blinked, annoyed. "Because you walked into the room."

He noticed what could only have been the wand of a genie box hanging limply from its cord over the lip of the nest. It was scratched and smeared with streaks of white guano. The box from which it unwound was propped among a clutch of eggs.

Leaf was hypnotized: this was the paintbrush whose stroke re ordered DNA, sculpted a new species, randomly ruined flesh, and granted living miracles. Yet it was so small, banal, a dirty utensil. It belonged among the broken bits of technology the birds collected. The pelican cleared her throat.

"No... I mean, why did you take me away from my boyfriend?"

And using that word for the first time in prison instead of under the sun, beside Scallop as they stepped from the sea, felt like a magic spell miscast, a song spent on deaf hearts.

"Oh." She seemed to sincerely consider her answer. Leaf wondered if taking care of so many eggs might have sparked the empathy the rest of her mutant species seemed to lack. "We collect and study as many of those touched by the wand as possible."

"Why?"

She guffawed and flicked at the dangling genie box wand. "To see what makes you tick! And you, especially. Your abilities have, uh, long-reaching possibilities."

"What do you mean?"

Weariness wrinkled her brow, "These eggs—most of our offspring are born dead or mangled. Maybe you can help?" With that, she reached behind her with her bill, scooped up a small, broken form, and pitched it toward him.

A ball of feathers punctuated by numerous sharp beaks rolled back and forth. Leaf thought it was dead until several beaks opened and closed in tandem, an effort to right itself. He stepped back to see all of the massive pelican as she shook her head in pity. He wanted to offer some words of comfort but noticed several boxes were set atop ceramic flower pots. The moist dirt they contained had failed to bud. The little army they had hoped to clone from him had failed to materialize.

He understood her pity was not for the abominations within the eggs but for him. He was worthless to them and justifiably expendable. He thought of the toasters, the VCRs, the boxes of phones he'd seen, and realized that to the pelicans, he was the same, another broken toy.

She readjusted her wings. "You think we are evil, but we are not. We are hungry. Evil is just an unappeasable hunger."

When he returned to his cage, a small white shell, a fragile scallop, had been set in the middle of the floor. He clutched it to his chest and felt the ridges of the shell press into his palm. He knew that the indentations carved the word "hope" into his flesh, and he squeezed tighter. He wondered if it would slip from his grasp, like Nanny's tooth that he had made into a necklace. He considered crushing it into powder and adding it to the water the guards brought him twice a day. Instead, he simply set it on the window sill. The message it carried had already reached his heart.

ONE AFTERNOON LEAF WAS SUMMONED to serve the pelicans alongside the consorts and dive boys who fed them their fish.

He had heard rumors of the King Pelicans' more transgressive habits, so he planned to make himself scarce as soon as possible.

Again the birds were assembled in the uppermost room of the aerie and clapped and guffawed as the dancing dive boys and flirtatious prostitutes pretended to tease them by withholding gasping fish. The trick was to taunt the birds without making them angry, as several slaves with a missing finger or two attested to the surly snap of their bills.

Distant thunder upset the birds. The pelicans flew about the room in a flurry of feathers. The sound, now louder, reverberated throughout the aerie. Slaves poured into the room, dressed in ruined tuxedos with frayed cuffs and shit-stained shoulders.

As the clouds darkened, each pelican waddled toward a slave and leaped up to roost on uniformly shaved heads. Rain fell silently outside as the birds tucked their bills under a wing and slept. Some even snored. One by one, the dive boys slunk from the room until only Leaf remained. He studied the slaves. Their faces were masks: blank, either from stupidity or surrender. The youngest regarded Leaf as well. Stout, well-muscled, his bare chest crossed with bands embroidered with little pelicans, he smiled at Leaf, his cheeks peppered with pimples and rolled his eyes upward at the human hand gripping his skull. Thunder rumbled outside. Delicately, he lifted the pelican off his head and slowly set him down on the floor. None of the other human pillars seemed to care. All of the pelicans were in a deep sleep.

The slave circled Leaf. From behind, he knowingly stroked Leaf's ribs and whispered in his ear. "They are afraid of the rain. They hate thunder."

Lightning cracked. Parched, Leaf ached for the rain. He wanted it to fill his mouth, cascade down his body, and fill the aerie so he could float away, carried down a river of silent grass.

Blunt fingertips pressed against his nipples. Leaf remembered that touch. "Gourd?"

"Yes. Don't worry, you won't be here long. You are so important to me—important to many of us." He pulled back one of the leather bands that crossed his chest to reveal a crude tattoo of a flower with Leaf's face beaming out of the center.

Gourd stroked the leaves at his neck with awe and affection. A pet to pelicans, a living rosary to others, Leaf had many questions for Gourd, but before he could say a word, the boy returned to his position and placed the sleeping bird back atop his head, then set a finger on Leaf's lips.

CODA

VISION

OUR BODIES WERE DRAGGED TO a clearing beside the canal and stacked like firewood. The green, glistening wall of the Everglades rose up on either side. I blinked as sunlight revived me. The men who pulled us from the barge moved with the same deliberate defeat. Their clothes were rags. Metal collars rusted around their wiry necks. I waited until they were gone before I pushed myself out of the pile of dead boys. I found Scallop, mouth open, sleeping a permanent sleep, dreaming of a big shark. I squatted by him and swatted away flies from his brow for about an hour, waiting for him to cough, to wake up. When another barge with bodies docked, I stepped into the swamp.

When the aerie was attacked under cover of a morning rainstorm, I was in my cell and, like the pelicans, mistook the bombs for thunder.

Bullets and cries of an uprising and hands pulled me into the hall. The crocodile kid lay dead and bloody on the floor. I opened my mouth to question my unseen saviors, but smoke poured down my throat, and

I choked and was pulled down the stairs and into the sunlight and saw Scallop. He was a graceful warrior, grinding his fishing spear into the deflated corpse of a fallen pelican. Sweat poured off him like the sea when I first saw him. But we were too far from each other. I tried to cry out but could only cough. A burning palm tree collapsed and sent fiery brush in all directions. I was shoved into the back of a waiting trunk among trembling pelican boys and the prone wounded. As they dropped a heavy tarp over us, I saw Scallop give his spear a final twist and trot toward the truck, toward his warm tomb and our last embrace. Too many shifting bodies, too tightly packed. I tried to shout but could only gasp as darkness enveloped us. I do not dream when I sleep, but I do exude large amounts of carbon dioxide.

While I slept, our deaths were discovered, and we were transferred to one of the many barges of the dead which flow up the canals, food for crops, fertilizer for pineapples, and detritus reclaimed by the great river that is the Everglades.

IN THE SWAMP, I STUMBLED through the brackish water and forded sawgrass. Blood seeped from fresh lacerations on my arms and thighs, grew viscous and sticky, sealed and reopened with fresh cuts. I walked until I was nearly submerged. Curious crocodiles with onyx eyes approached and turned away, disdainful of my vegetable state.

I pierced my foot all the way through on the sharp rising root of a black mangrove and walked. The wound closed around black soil.

Dirt tumbled through my bloodstream and wound its way through my veins. I tasted decay.

So I stood still.

I opened my pores to the bitter tannin tea of crushed leaf and general rot. I lifted particles of soil into me from the soles of my butchered and weary feet. Having lived a life on sand and clean ground made of sparkling bits of bone and shell, I had never before stood in such dark soil. Unadulterated earth fed me as the sun. A diet of death. And finally, I cried and screamed and still needed more pain, something physical to match the ache that swung around my shrinking heart like a raging, cancerous moon. I clutched my shoulder, dug my nails into grieving flesh, tore off my right arm, and flung it toward two motley vultures who had eyed my journey thus far with little interest. They flapped heavy wings and repositioned themselves on a nearby branch. The arm floated like driftwood. My distant hand spasmodically flexed an empty grip. As the arm settled into the murky water, a black snake slithered between its green fingers. Jade blood pumped out of the fresh stump as I staggered and swooned. And unconsciously healed myself. Against my will, I basked the wound in sunlight and felt new emerging flesh strain sunward. I so yearn for light.

I continued to feed on black nutrients as I stood there, rooted. I continued to weep as the sun set and welcomed the gloom of sleep.

I did not move when I woke but cried more green tears. I cried all day. So many tears flowed that a sticky amber soon erased my mouth, crystallizing off my chin in a forked stalactite. The smoldering orange of dusk settled across the Everglades, and I closed my eyes, hoping that I would cry through the night and wake up a crystal tree, an impervious gem.

Day again, and I stood still, rooted, literally rooted to the ground.

I had sunk roots into the moist earth during the night, pushing new parts of myself into the soil, tasting ancient compacted rot, and absorbing primordial, wet knowledge. Unknowingly, thus rooted, I had begun to grow again.

As I grew, my sadness grew within as well. Tears continued to deform my face. The sun rose and set countless times. One morning I was startled from my permanent grief as a flock of stilt-like flamingos took flight from my shoulders. They poured over the rising sun like a silken caress. There were hundreds of them. It was time to take stock: my arm had re-grown but was a well-muscled dark wood, armored with the thick bark of experience. My discarded arm had climbed to a nearby ridge of high growth and planted itself. It sat there like a gigantic log. Bright green roots flowed forth from its socket and sank into the ground. I realized I was looking down at it from high above.

So I am monolithic. I thought to take a step but realized I was rooted too deeply; I had allowed myself to spread far below the muck and into the aquifer. I drank cool, perfect water that flowed between the skull and skin of the world. I concentrated, and my green arm shivered with a coat of new leaf. I flexed my brown arm and turned the flesh from oak to cypress. I pulled water up from underground and allowed it to settle in my mouth. I parted my lips, snapping the strands of mangrove that had sewn my mouth shut. Egrets settled in this grotto. I expanded underground until I reached a portion of the everglades poisoned by kudzu. Interesting: the plant had the same taste as the fuel those crafty pelicans used to spin electricity.

As if on cue, the men came. Soldiers from the Kudzu Army came to cut me down. Axes above their heads, they chopped at my ankles.

I splintered as I changed what type of wood I was at the point of entry, absorbing some blows while deflecting others, sending menacing mangrove spikes up through the soil until I was protected by a field of thorns. They tried to burn me, and I turned my flesh into the greenest bamboo. And before they struck again, I pulled at the water beneath the soil; I spread the great leaves at my neck to absorb as much light as possible, and I grew even more. I grew so fast that I absorbed some men as they tried to escape. I took them inside me and slowly, lovingly, tenderly dissolved them, minutely appreciating every bit of nourishment they provided. I sifted out their bones and weapons and expelled them from my bowels. Tree rats scratched at this shiny pile but eventually abandoned it, their stomachs empty.

By now, I had grown until I reached my discarded arm. I hoisted it up, snapping its stringy roots, and added it to the center of my chest, a vital appendage with an upturned hand beckoning more sun. I filled the palm with the giant disc of a solitary sunflower. Colonies of bees propagated in the grooves of the fingertips of my third hand. They measured out honey in their tireless combs, and countless drones risked the wind to take nectar from the plants that laced the terraces of my ribs, but my sympathies were with the unseen queens.

And I grew until the remnants of some government somewhere sent two helicopters to observe. I was still intent on the ecstatic tickle of several thousand bees pulling pollen from my sunflower. The machines eventually gained the courage to come closer. When they did, I turned and opened my mouth to reveal the paradise I contained: a splendid sanctuary surrounded the sandbar of my tongue.

Albino alligators lazed in the sun. Pink flamingos napped as golden cattails whispered between my teeth. I silently mocked these graceless floppy metallic mosquitoes by burping giant tender dandelions into the air. I raised my oaken arm in a swatting gesture, and the helicopters fled. Interesting that the King Pelicans never came. Not once did they come to take stock, even at a distance. They are happy to tuck their bills under their wings and ignore me. I grant them the same respect.

THE TIDES OF NIGHT AND day consumed a considerable amount of time, and I continued to grow. A solitary man pushed through the bush. I knew him from miles away; my roots read the prints of his bare and butchered soles. Hardy wearily approached. I reached out to him, extending several vines that ended in the delicate hands he would remember. I gently touched him, and he shuddered, recoiled in guilt. He pivoted and collapsed, whimpering, tired, and sad. I pressed one of my many palms to his chest and realized that his scales had hardened so that no heartbeat could be felt. I put a finger in his mouth and tasted sour drugs, soul-deadening chemicals; the pollutants he had taken to submerge his pain had nearly drowned him. Parched, he sucked at my finger. I changed it to a life-giving nipple and fed him white nectar. He relaxed as I lifted him up into the air and into my mouth.

He slept on my tongue—an exhausted soldier relieved of duty. I exuded a soft grass to massage him, treat the cuts from the sawgrass, and lovingly sucked out the tiny infections which dotted his skin. I drank the ink from his bad tattoos. When he awoke, he stripped off his filthy torn shorts and dove into the pool of rainwater I had collected in my grotto-mouth. As he swam, I warmed the water and let him sweat out his grief and confusion. He crawled onto my tongue and lay on his back like a gleeful infant as I sent vines to caress him, feed him, enter him, milk him, envelope him and slowly spin him in the air, extending him out of my mouth and above the swamp shimming below. He cooed in awe as curious birds banked to land on the forest of my shoulders. I rhythmically expanded the stalk planted in his anus as he stretched and moaned. I opened a mouth in the palm of one of my hands and sampled the seed he spilled across his scarred stomach. He still tasted like tomorrow, and I loved him for it.

I sent a tiny, tender root up his nose and carefully caressed his brain. I found lesions and burns from the chemicals he had ingested and salved them with a healing mixture of my saliva, blood, and semen. I tightened the minuscule vine into a small noose and severed the tiny part of his mind that knew regret. I swallowed this bland morsel, and Hardy curled into a deep, untroubled sleep, and I brought him back into my mouth to rest.

More people came, this time to worship. Reformed dive boys, fishermen, escaped slaves, and young mothers with infants. I ignored them as they set up camp, keeping their fires small lest they offend me, respecting the Everglades, fishing only what they needed, and weaving living huts of grass. I paid them no mind until they paid me in music.

One day, as the sun set, a boy took up a drum, and I slowly turned my head for the first time in months. They supplicated themselves in ecstasy and showed me their upraised palms with my beaming face painted in the center. More drumming began. I spread my arms and launched a thousand birds. A colony of fruit bats rustled within my armpits, annoyed at the surprising shock of sunlight. Emboldened, men and women rushed me and climbed the massive banyan trees of my ankles. My stamen unfurled for the first time since I had become the Everglades. Its wavering shadow cooled the sweating drummers. Music vibrated within; I further engorged. Hundreds prayed to my rising and put their hands to the earth as I showered them with heavy warm seed. They groveled and smeared the humid bliss on each other's bodies. They began to copulate in the cooling pools. Hardy swung from my bottom lip and cheered them on with simian hoots. They drank me like animals as the last drops fell to earth. I reabsorbed the seed into my roots, and they furiously dug into the earth to follow it down. I opened my roots to swallow their heads and hands, and they eagerly joined me, burrowing farther, shoulder to shoulder, kicking their legs up into the air to force themselves underground. The men and women and children at my ankles clamored to secrete themselves into the hollows of my flesh. I parted my skin and opened my veins to gloss them with my blood.

Flowing amber encased them in serene ecstasy. I erased their eyes so they could fully concentrate on becoming part of me. I allowed them to flow across the fields of my thighs, settling them within pockets of soft tubers to be nurtured and changed so they, too, could be suckled by the sun.

Forever awake, careful not to blink and dislodge the papery white orchids and veins of orange bougainvillea that pour from my tear ducts, I have a few more miles to go before I breach the atmosphere and spread my canopy. I am vast and can lick starlight. The stars are the flavor of morning dew condensing on the night side of pregnant blueberries. Stars. They sound distant sapphire notes, whale songs sung by blind immortal beasts that still somehow die. I see how they cluster and flow with the galactic tide. And I see that, like a smile, space curves.

EXCERPT FROM THE 2013
LAMBDA LITERARY AWARD
ACCEPTANCE SPEECH BY
TOM CARDAMONE:

I WOULD LIKE TO SAY THAT WE
ARE ALL SCIENCE FICTION
AND FANTASY AUTHORS.

ALL OF US WERE GIVEN A STORY OF SHAME
AND ISOLATION AND RE-WROTE IT.

WE IMAGINED BETTER FUTURES AND
MADE THEM HAPPEN.

AND MAYBE THAT IS OUR DESTINY.

NOW THAT WE HAVE LEARNED TO
ADVOCATE FOR OURSELVES,
WE MUST ADVOCATE FOR
OTHERS.

TOM CARDAMONE

is the editor of *Crashing Cathedrals: Edmund White by the Book* and co-editor of *Fever Spores: The Queer Reclamation of William S. Burroughs* and is the author of the Lambda Literary Award finalist erotic novel *The Lurid Sea*. Among other works, he is the author of two short story collections, *Night Sweats: Tales of Homosexual Wonder and Woe* and *Pumpkin Teeth*, which was also a Lambda finalist.

MICHAEL BUKOWSKI

has been a freelance illustrator for twenty years, predominantly working for punk and metal bands on five continents. Most notably, he was the "head of propaganda" for the Philly-based, anarcho-hardcore band R.A.M.B.O., helping them craft a ridiculous aesthetic for their print-based materials, as well as providing props for live shows around the world. Since the turn of the century, Michael has amassed a client list of over 200 bands, labels, production companies, and clothing lines. More recently he's worked with weird fiction authors and publishers on covers, interior illustrations, in addition to the essay series Stories From the Borderland with Scott Nicolay. His Illustro Obscurum project, in which he is illustrates creatures and entities from prominent horror and weird fiction writers, led to him founding the small press zine "publishing house" Seventh Church Ministries, which showcases other illustrators' work alongside famous (or not-so-famous) authors. While based in Philadelphia, Michael is also an avid taphophile and traveller; he regularly visits remote cemeteries, ancient ruins, ossuaries, and tombstone festivals with his partner and fellow illustrator, Jeanne D'Angelo. He's also the father to three annoying cats.